W9-CJS-407

MY   R443197
                            12.95
bringle   Sep88
Murder most gentrified

*Murder Most
Gentrified*

By Mary Bringle

Murder Most Gentrified

MARY BRINGLE

CRIME CLUB
Doubleday
NEW YORK   LONDON   TORONTO   SYDNEY

All of the characters in this book
are fictitious, and any resemblance
to actual persons, living or dead,
is purely coincidental.

A Crime Club Book
Published by Doubleday, a division of
Bantam Doubleday Dell Publishing Group, Inc.
666 Fifth Avenue, New York, New York 10103

Doubleday and the portrayal of a man with a gun are trademarks of Doubleday,
a division of Bantam Doubleday Dell Publishing Group, Inc.

Library of Congress Cataloging-in-Publication Data

Bringle, Mary.
Murder most gentrified/Mary Bringle.
p.   cm.
I. Title.
PS3552.R485M8   1988
813'.54—dc19   87-35205

ISBN 0-385-24331-6

OG

For Robin and Willie and Stain

"Just think how much this will increase the value of property around here!"

—Overheard on an elevator the day after John Lennon was shot

*Murder Most
Gentrified*

ONE

The prospect of taking a restorative bath, dressing in the candy-striped flannel nightgown which so reminded her of childhood, and sinking into immediate sleep—badly needed sleep at that—was not attractive. For one thing, it was only early evening in New York, and she would surely waken sometime after midnight with the unappetizing small hours of the night to be traversed. It would be too late to call friends, and she had nothing to read. She had read and reread the many books in the second bedroom, which had been turned into a study, and she knew from experience that fresh reading material was needed to combat jet lag.

Scooping the contents of her suitcase onto her living room floor, Sarah began to sort the garments into piles for the laundry hamper and piles for the cleaner. The apartment building seemed unnaturally quiet, but street noises insinuated their way up to her seventh-floor fastness with an irritating regularity she had almost forgotten. The blasting sirens and whooping, self-important bleats of ambulettes were a constant, of course, but for the first time she noticed the frequency with which automobile burglar alarms made their bid to join the little symphony. When had they become so ubiquitous?

Well, you experienced a trade-off when a neighborhood became gentrified. Instead of the jolly shrieks and murderous howls which had once floated up from the welfare hotels at either end of Sarah's block, she was now treated to the screams of glee of well-fed young people who poured from the doors of sushi parlors on nearby Columbus Avenue. The bracing sounds of a shattering pint of Thunderbird had been replaced, in warm weather, by the cacophony of street musicians. There were brass bands and string quartets, mimes and fire-eaters, tap dancers who jittered away on tatty squares of cardboard. There had even been, last summer, a portly fortune-teller who set up her card table and folding chair outside a popular Cuban restaurant. There had also been an untalented player of the marimba, who beat out the two tunes he had committed to memory with a dogged zeal Sarah might have found touching if she had not had to live in the same neighborhood.

But this was January. Winter. The street musicians had temporarily gone into hiding. It was the time when mysterious notes from the super appeared in the building's elevator, notes in which the super seemed to wish to be apologetic. *Maybe going to be no hot water,* these missives warned. Or, *Keep cold water running all night! Chot off hot water, or maybe going to freeze!*

No such warning had greeted her on her return from London. Instead, fastened in the little window to the left of the elevator, she had blearily read: *The Board of Directors wishes to invite all Shareholders to a party for the purpose of airing grievances and furthering community cooperation! Wine and Cheese! Thank you for not Smoking!*

Sarah, oppressed by the notion of herself as a *shareholder,* abandoned the sorting of her garments and rose to her feet. She would go to the lovable bookstore, select a new novel by the Australian writer she most admired, and defeat jet lag in one way or another. Standing at her brass coat tree, she decided on a heavy woolen jacket and a matching pair of angora gloves and beret purchased from a street vendor, and fled into the dim outer hall, hoping to meet nobody.

Outside, under the building's new canopy, it was bitterly cold. Across the street she could see an old party being ladled into an ambulette. Swiveling uneasily to her right, she saw the heavily padded figure of one of her fellow shareholders advancing relentlessly, bearing down on her with a proprietary smile.

"When did you get back from your travels?" asked Mr. Crotty, beaming now and emitting little plumes of frosty breath.

"About an hour ago," said Sarah. She hoped that Mr. Crotty would understand that she was jet-lagged and withdraw with a neighborly nod. But Mr. Crotty was a recent widower, and lonely, and capable of sustaining very long conversations.

"Enjoyed yourself?" he asked. Before Sarah could answer he slapped his gloved hands together and embarked on a detailed description of the water damage his ceilings had succumbed to during her absence. "Everybody always thinks it's such a picnic, living on the top floor. Nobody overhead, am I right? But let me tell you—living on the top floor means endless grief, as far as your ceilings go. Damage to the roof? Damage to your ninth-floor ceiling, and that's a fact. Mine looks like a pizza. Just above the north-facing windows? A pizza—stains and blobs and little flaky chips drifting down."

"What a shame," murmured Sarah, trying to picture how the flaky chips figured in the pizza image. "I suppose someone on the Board has had a look at it?"

"The Board!" cried Mr. Crotty scornfully. "The Board's the enemy, Sarah! Shall I tell you what I think? I think all those plants on the penthouse terrace are the root of all our roof troubles."

Approximately two thirds of the shareholders had expressed concern over the dense foliage being maintained on the roof, but surely this was a summer problem? Sarah's fingertips testified to the fact that this was winter, and although she sympathized with Mr. Crotty's water damage and had often wondered at the wisdom of keeping a jungle on the roof, she felt it was unfair, on her first day back, to be hurtled into a discussion of the building's never-ending problems.

She was saved by the sudden appearance of a brisk investment banker, a new neighbor who had bought 5A after poor Tess Abelson collapsed in an aisle of Food World and died. The investment banker—Miss Johnson? Miss Jacobs?—slid between Sarah and Mr. Crotty with a tense smile and plunged her key into the lock. Mr. Crotty followed her into the building, not wishing to miss the elevator.

Sarah walked quickly to the corner and became a part of the ceaseless migration which is Columbus Avenue. Women in huge-shouldered furs impeded her progress. They had a distressing habit of stopping suddenly, in front of lighted shop windows, so that Sarah nearly tripped over them. Bulky purses and sports bags nudged her in ways she found offensive. Where was it written that she, who had lived in this neighborhood when it was little more than a slum, should have to be poked by the squash racquettes of the upwardly mobile?

Turning breathlessly at the main artery, Sarah tried to plot her course. It was disorienting. The old Chinese restaurant she had patronized for more than a decade was now an overpriced ice cream emporium. The stationery place, where she had once purchased humble items like typing paper and Ko-Rec-Type, had been reborn as a shop where one might purchase cowboy boots made from the skins of endangered species. The streets of her neighborhood literally changed overnight, and since she had been away for a month, they seemed even more unfamiliar. She counted to herself: card shop, still with us. Deli also, but with suspicious signs of new, upscale renovation. Shoe repair shop, gone. Replaced with underwear boutique featuring hundred-dollar silk teddies. Dry-cleaning store boarded up and displaying a "We Lost Our Lease" sign. She could see a small knot of people clustering at the window of what she hoped would still be the bookstore, and walked faster.

The window which drew the crowd was oddly backlit, indicating that the store was not open for business, since all was dark inside. It took Sarah a few moments to insinuate her way to the front of the crowd. Several people were giggling, but the rest were shaking their heads and making sounds of resigned disgust.

In the display case, someone had placed a plaster skeleton, the kind used for Halloween parties. The cavernous eye sockets and bony rictus were regarding a book held in the skeleton's unpleasantly long fingers. The skeleton was reading, obviously, but what was the meaning of it? The store's clerks had often shown a penchant for the bizarre, and in October the little tableau might have been quite appropriate, but now?

"Lost their lease, probably," offered a bookish-looking young man. "Death knell for the bookstore."

"What next?" inquired an untidy woman in a dusty down coat. "Another boutique we don't need and can't afford."

Sarah chose to walk back via Broadway, avoiding the ordeal of Columbus Avenue. At the newsstand she bought several magazines she did not want to read and gave a polite member of the homeless some change, realizing too late that the coins were English, a relic of her recent sojourn in London. The memory of the skeleton in her favorite bookstore combined with the malaise of jet lag, and when a neighbor, entering the elevator at the fifth floor, began to speak of troubles with the building's boiler, she was almost rude.

The building was a standard West Side item—nine floors of large, prewar apartments, four apartments to each floor, two professional apartments at the street level, and two penthouses on the roof. The lobby was eccentric, sporting black and white tiles and a crimson Art Deco elevator which was always breaking down. In the old days, before the building had reluctantly gone co-op, the amenities had consisted of three pieces of wrought-iron garden furniture and one large, standing ashtray, all securely bolted to the floor.

Now comfortable leather armchairs had replaced the garden suite, and a large potted plant reigned over the ashtray's old spot. Thin walnut paneling had been introduced, and new, larger mailboxes to accommodate the huge influx of junk mail each of the shareholders now received daily.

As yet there was no doorman, although the new people plainly ached for one. It could be said that the building was in a state of war, although it was a restrained sort of battle. On the one hand were the original inhabitants, who saw a doorman as the final nail in their coffins; on the other hand were the new shareholders, who could not be made to understand that people still existed—here and now in the latter quarter of the twentieth century—who would be driven from their homes by the raise in maintenance a doorman would ensure.

Mr. Crotty was trying to put these sentiments into a letter on the evening of Sarah's return. He saw it as a humane and sociological document, his letter, which would be read into the minutes of the next meeting of the Board of Directors. The letter, though, was threatening to defeat him. Just when it was shaping up, exciting him, he would go off on wild tangents, feeling the need to expand on certain details. A will independent of his own made him chronicle the long and pleasant life he and Mrs. Crotty had enjoyed on the premises, rearing two children. Even as he wrote, secure at the kitchen table where Kitty had so often produced unwanted meals, he sensed the useless nature of his enterprise.

"Give it up, Tim," he told himself, and went to another room to pour himself a generous drink of whiskey.

Milagros woke abruptly to an unfamiliar sound. It was a faint but persistent noise, and it seemed to be coming from a place directly above her head. She sat up in bed and concentrated. Who could be tapping away up there, like a prisoner communicating in code? The woman who lived in the apartment upstairs had been away for several weeks, hadn't she? And, even if she had returned, why should she be making this noise at—Milagros consulted her alarm clock—three in the morning?

It was a burglar, then. The thought of a burglar would have made her shiver, but it was difficult to shiver in the overheated atmosphere of the maid's room. She knew it was called a maid's room because Jewel, one of the other au pairs, had told her so. Milagros did not like the designation, but you could hardly call the space the au pair room. Nanny room was nicer. All in all, she was quite pleased with her quarters. The room was off beyond the kitchen, at maximum distance from the Adlers, her employers, and the two little girls she minded. There was just room for the single bed, a dresser, and the night table, and beyond was her own half-bath. Half-bath was exactly the right description for it, because the bath was exactly half as big as a normal American tub. It had a wonderful nozzle device which could be employed for the washing of hair, when the water pressure wasn't acting up. Best of all, Milagros had her own toilet, with a padded cushion that released a soft sigh when she plumped down on it.

She had written to her mother, in Honduras, about the unusual toilet seat, and that had been a big mistake. Her mother had fired back an urgent warning, explaining how the toilet seat was a possible agent of evil, and urging Milagros to oil it with the meat of an avocado on the night of the new moon. Her mother was a *bruja*, and a woman to be reckoned with, but somehow her power became reduced in written words. How could she explain to her that in the supermarkets of New York the avocados were usually cold and firm—unripe? Or that if Milagros were to purchase a hard avocado and let it ripen in her room, she would be defying the Adlers' house rules?

The tapping noises had ceased, and all thoughts of creeping out to the kitchen and dialing 911 on the wall phone, asking the police to investigate, had vanished. Instead, Milagros thought she might make one of her secret tours of the apartment. She had done it only twice in the six months she had spent in the Adlers' nanny room. A daytime tour was more satisfactory, of course, because she could penetrate every room, but the opportunities for a daytime tour were few and far between. Only once had the entire Adler family been absent—an occasion when Megan and Phoebe had been obliged to accompany their parents to a funeral for their grandmother—and on that day Milagros had wandered from room to room like an indolent queen. She had imagined that she was the owner of this urban paradise, pressing the blender's buttons in the kitchen to hear them sing, pretending to strum the keys of the piano in the living room (Mrs. Adler had once cherished hopes of being a concert pianist), and seating herself at the head of the table in the green-papered dining room.

The bedrooms were harder to invade. She had ignored the all-too-familiar sleeping places of Megan and Phoebe, and gone to the forbidden zone. The Adlers' bedroom was completely carpeted in blue wool, and it was much bigger than a bedroom ought to be; it had all the usual things and still had space for a chintz-covered chaise longue and a large television set. What really made the room magical for Milagros was the ice-blue comforter that covered the king-size bed. It shimmered, looking silvery and cold, but it was wonderfully warm and soft to the touch. Milagros had lain on it, planting herself in the exact center of the bed, staring at the creamy ceiling. She had allowed herself to think *All this belongs to me*, and for a time the feeling was so heady she felt almost paralyzed by it. If the Adlers had returned at that moment, she doubted very much that she would have been able to move.

The tapping sound returned, and suddenly she knew that she was hearing a typewriter. She knew that the woman upstairs must have returned, because a thief would hardly be typing. Milagros had slept through far worse noise and, rejecting the idea of a tour, she burrowed back beneath the covers. She thought of a new way she might arrange her hair, and pictured the reaction she would get from Jewel and the other au pairs when they met, with their charges, the next day in Central Park. Jewel and Noreen, the other West Indian girl, had nappy hair and would be envious, but it was the reaction of Teresa she most looked forward to. Teresa was an illegal from Ireland, and she had recently maimed her beautiful strawberry hair by cutting off a foot of it and forcing it into punkish spikes.

Milagros smiled in the dark, touching her own hair for luck. It was good Indian hair, thick and straight and black as tar. As she was slipping back into sleep, she thought of someone else who would be annoyed by her new hairstyle. Mrs. Adler was a nice-looking woman, and she certainly made the best of her God-given attributes, but her hair was fine and lusterless. She wore it short, like a puny little cap, and washed it every day.

Musing on her employer's hair, Milagros fell asleep. The noises overhead reached a crescendo some forty minutes later, and then faded. They were replaced by the almost comically loud din of the garbage compactors which serviced the restaurants along Columbus Avenue, and then, for a little time before dawn, it was silent.

TWO

The shareholders' party was held in the lobby, for lack of a better place. In the past, the building had always held parties along more traditionally friendly lines—cocktails in one apartment, potluck dinner in another, and coffee and dessert in a third. Strange, now that they were a co-op, the spirit of cooperation had come to an end. As tenants they had all been friends, except for a few holdouts; now that they had become elevated to the status of shareholders, they were too busy thinking of their apartments as investments which must be guarded, improved, and—in some cases—not examined too closely.

There were extensive renovations going on in several of the apartments, and since each structural change had to be approved by the Board of Directors, certain people were behaving rather secretively. Then, too, with the influx of new families that had bought apartments at the staggering "outsider" price, the old tenants scarcely knew who was a neighbor and who a contractor, delivery boy, or city engineer.

"This is worse than a gallery opening," said Maryanne Francini (5A) to Sarah Mason (7B).

"You mean the bad wine?" asked Sarah, lifting a plastic cup of New York white and saluting.

But Maryanne seemed disinclined to pursue the topic. "How was your trip to London?"

"Not bad," said Sarah. She was aware that she ought to offer more, but she knew that Maryanne was preoccupied and wouldn't really listen to what she had to say. Maryanne was a photographer's rep who worked out of her apartment, and Sarah was a free-lance journalist. In a word, they were self-employed and barely holding on. They had each moved into their six-room apartments as the gallant wives of established husbands. In the good old days they could afford to be self-employed. There was even a certain cachet attached to their status, which had mysteriously disappeared along with their husbands. Formerly, they had been the daring half of an otherwise conventional couple, but now?

Sarah was struggling to put a frame to her new status when she felt a tweaking at her back.

"So!" cried Mrs. Strabinski of the sixth floor rear. "How goes it with the world traveler? How is it with the great writer?" She smiled up at Sarah, displaying dazzling bridgework framed by the cherry-colored lipstick she had loyally worn for fifty years. In the next moment, she pulled Sarah close to her well-padded bosom and lowered one eyelid in a conspirator's wink.

"Listen," she muttered, speaking out of the corner of her mouth like a movie gangster. "Listen, Sarah. The one who bought the apartment overhead, you know who I mean, she's planning to sell *immediately!* She's modernizing her kitchen, and I have the water damage in my hall closet to prove it! She's a profiter—no worse, she's a profiteer! A pirate!"

The elevator doors parted and Mr. Crotty made an entrance, clutching a folding chair. Had he confused the event? Did he think the shareholders' party was a replay of the long, boring meetings when they had all hunched in the lobby, voicing their protests against the concept of ownership? The long trestle table which had been set up to accommodate the plastic glasses and gallons of wine and the plates of Finnish flatbread and wheels of upscale cheese was, to be sure, the same table which lawyers and real estate cowboys and dandruff-shouldered managing agents had once commandeered in order to coax the backward tenants.

"No better than a pirate," hissed Ida Strabinski, relinquishing Sarah's arm. "Think about it."

"Security," came a deep voice on the other side of the table. "What about security? I can't believe there are people in this building who wouldn't be glad to spend, say, fifty dollars in maintenance per month for a doorman."

"Some of us can't afford what we're paying now," said Maryanne. "Some of us would find a doorman a real pain in the ass."

"You can't afford to get complacent about crime, can you?"

"I can," said Maryanne. "Listen up, mister. This co-op had the first all-gay Board of Directors ever. Does that sound so dangerous to you?"

The lobby was swiftly filling up. The President of the Board of Directors, a suave man with a spade-shaped beard, sat beneath the mailboxes, granting interviews for all the world as if he were a Godfather of the Mafia. The Recording Secretary chipped away at the cheese and laughed impartially, and others worked the room as if they had been born for a political life, pumping hands and feigning interest in their neighbors' problems.

"Have you met the Adlers yet, Sarah?" Monica Platt was indicating a tall, thin couple. The female Adler was dressed in regulation Wall Street attire, but out of deference to the festivity of the occasion she had chosen a bright red silk blouse. She looked a bit uneasy, but that could be explained by the presence of Monica, a relentlessly vivacious woman who never used a simple word when a fancier one would do. Sarah suspected that Monica was the only member of the board who actually *enjoyed* her duties.

"This is Ruth Adler," Monica said, "and her spouse is Joe. They used to reside in Park Slope, didn't you, Ruth?"

"Yes," said Ruth Adler. "Hello, Sarah."

"Those two adorable little girls are their children," said Monica. "You know the ones I mean. You see them in the elevator with their governess."

"I wouldn't exactly call Milagros a governess," said Joe Adler, with the hint of a smile. "She's more a kind of live-in baby-sitter."

While Sarah uttered pleasantries she called up the image of the baby-sitter as she had seen her that very day on the elevator. Milagros was a small, compact girl with glowing dark skin and a heartbreakingly childish smile. She had the look of one who was both naive and knowing, if such a thing were possible. Her abundant black hair had been dressed beautifully so that she sported a little crown of thick braids and a shiny swag down the back. It was a fashion statement which gloated: *I may be a small, brown person from a Third World country, but I have hair to spare!*

"She's a sweet kid," Joe Adler said, while his wife smiled thinly.

"The baby-sitter's country of origin is Honduras," said Monica. She had a way of pursing her lips after each statement, as if she had ingested a morsel of food.

"Oh ho!" cried Mr. Crotty, who had stowed his folding chair under the stairs and come to join them. "I have a tale to tell." There was a speck of cheese fixed to his chin, and he grasped his glass of wine so tightly Sarah feared it might break. The Adlers moved back almost imperceptibly.

"This is Mr. Crotty," explained Monica, "of whom I can say I have had the pleasure of being acquainted with him for twenty-five years."

"What's your tale, Mr. Crotty?" Joe Adler's tone of voice was professionally pitched, not quite condescending.

Sarah, fearing to hear once more about water damage, had prepared to flee. Her body had turned. She had begun to make eye contact with Maryanne so that she might pretend to take up an interrupted conversation, but Mr. Crotty's words forced her to reconsider.

"Now that window," he was saying, "is a form of terrorism. I'm not condemning it, but let's see it for what it is. They're fighting back, the only way they know how, and with the only resources they have."

"Why fight progress?" murmured Joe Adler. "It's an exercise in futility, isn't it?"

"Progress?" roared Mr. Crotty. "What on earth does that mean? Some greedy bastard decides he can make hundreds of thousands instead of a perfectly sweet amount of tens of thousands by grinding people down? He's gonna close down a useful business to replace it with something nobody needs? He's gonna decide no one needs books anymore, but they all need sneakers the price would pay the rent a few years back? I ask you, and no offense young fella, is that what you call *progress?*"

"Are you talking about the skeleton in the bookstore?" asked Sarah. "The one reading a book?"

Mr. Crotty's fanatic eyes locked gratefully on hers and seemed to clear. "No, honey," he said. "The skeleton's not reading any-more. This war has escalated."

The skeleton was now, in fact, snorting coke. Someone had dressed him in a Coca-Cola T-shirt and placed a mirror with three lines of white powder, neatly cut, between his sprawling femurs. A straw had been shoved into one of his yawning nasal cavities.

"That's awfully ugly," Maryanne said almost reverently. "Really hideous."

Sarah, shivering, agreed.

"Probably what that is is talcum powder," said a teenaged girl. "Or it could be, like, Tide." She looked as if she might be prepared to smash the window to find out, but the window was unsmashable and the store fitted out with many alarms.

"I think I need a drink," said Maryanne. "My place or yours?"

"Mine," said Sarah. "I have some duty-free."

They headed back for the apartment building, having long ago forsaken the bars of Columbus Avenue. It was cheaper, and more reassuring, to have a drink at home. The lobby was empty and bore no signs of the dismal little party they had so recently vacated. The older folks, like Monica and Mr. Crotty, had no doubt left with reluctance, while the young professionals would have ridden the elevator back to their apartments gratefully, eager to prepare themselves for another day of work. Sarah and Maryanne, who fell between the groups by reason of age and rank in the world, felt caught in a limbo.

Their apartments were identical in layout and similar in spirit. Rooms intended for family living were relegated to strictly practical purposes. The formal dining room, which Sarah now slept in, was Maryanne's office. Sarah's principal bedroom had become a sort of storage space, bristling with old files and dusty crates and Xeroxed copies of her articles in limp manila envelopes. Her maid's room, where she did her writing, contained a washer and dryer, relics of her marriage for which she felt thankful. Maryanne's had been converted to a darkroom.

"What's the pattern?" Maryanne sipped at her duty-free whiskey, which she liked to overwhelm with club soda and ice. "Why does he go from reading to snorting?"

"More upscale," said Sarah. "More suitable to the neighborhood?"

"Nahh. This isn't a Yuppie statement we've got here. This is a protest. Did you hear what old Crotty said? 'This war has escalated.' He sees it as a war, Sarah, not as some visual *statement*. Somebody is pissed to hell about the bookstore closing, and some landlord salivating because he can see a two-hundred-percent profit, and—" Maryanne flung a hand in the air. "You're the writer," she said. "Take it from there."

"Right," said Sarah, feeling the good taste of the whiskey washing away the pissy one of the shareholders' party. "Whoever is setting up that display case is someone who wants to make a point. Who can afford the prices along the strip? That pizza place—the one that moved in when the Greek luncheonette was forced out of business? I heard they're paying eighteen thousand dollars a month."

"You'd have to move a lot of pizza to come up with that."

"Exactly my point! All these little boutiques and never-neverland shops. Why do they exist?"

"To service Yuppies," said Maryanne.

"But most of the time they're practically empty," said Sarah. "I've never seen Mrs. Dress-for-Success Adler handing over her Platinum Amex to buy a lilac smoking jacket for her husband."

"Tax shelters? Shelters for drug-runners? Laundering money?"

"That suggests Swiss bank accounts. I've never quite grasped what 'laundering money' meant. Have you?"

Maryanne shook her head in a martyred fashion. "All I know," she said, "is that things are getting weird out there. I wish I were a million miles away from Columbus Avenue."

"Amen," said Sarah.

If she turned the tap water down a bit, Milagros thought she'd be able to overhear some of the conversation from the dining room. She was scraping carrots for Phoebe and Megan's healthful snack, the one they always enjoyed after Megan's afternoon nap. The voices of Mrs. Adler and the funny old lady from the sixth floor carried quite well, and Milagros grew alert as she heard the word "rape" being mentioned.

"How awful," Mrs. Adler was saying. "Did you ever see the girls again?"

"No, no. Immediately they're whisked away. You can understand, after such an ordeal."

Milagros thought the old lady was from Germany, or one of those countries in Europe, because her English was not proper. She said *visked avay*.

"But my point," said the old lady, "is that we used to be a Target Crime Area." She said the words importantly, as if proud to have been a target, even if it had been a long time ago. "We can't afford to feel so secure, just because the neighborhood's so much better. It could happen again!"

Mrs. Adler said something about a doorman, and Milagros grinned, because she understood exactly how the conversation would go from this point on. She had lived in the nanny room long enough to see how the lines were drawn. The new people and the old people wanted to get along, but there was a fundamental difference between them. The new people, like her employers, believed that every problem could be resolved with money. The old people—and some of them were not, strictly speaking, old—had very little money and were afraid of being overwhelmed, voted down, and driven out.

Milagros understood many things, and among them was the reason that Mrs. Adler had settled in the dining room for her conversation with the European lady. She hoped to make the interview as brief as possible and still seem hospitable. Mrs. A's time was precious. She went out to business three days a week, and was preparing to return on a full-time basis now that her little girls were four and seven, respectively, and she had Milagros to help. She also understood that Phoebe and Megan much preferred the sweet known as M&M's to the strips of celery and carrot they were so regularly given on awaking, but bribing the children was a tricky business. Phoebe could be depended upon, bitch though she was, whereas Megan, the younger and more innocent, the one Milagros was soft on, might conceivably blow her cover.

She gathered the orange carrot peelings in her fingers and conveyed them to the coffee can she used for small garbage. From the dining room, she could hear the voice of the quaint one, who was arguing for a TV surveillance system they could all afford.

"It seems rather a half-measure," Mrs. Adler said, and Milagros could imagine the little perpendicular wrinkle between her eyebrows. Phoebe would have one like it when she grew up.

"Not necessarily!" cried the other. "It seems Allen and Douglas once had something similar in their old building, something responsible for a *reduction in crime.*"

Allen and Douglas were *maricóns* who lived together on the third floor. There were quite a few *maricóns* living in the building—she had counted at least two male couples, and there were possibly others she hadn't yet met. One was supposed to feel a mild contempt for them, men who were not really men, but Milagros had discovered that she liked them. They seemed gentle and friendly, and they laughed easily and always helped her if she was having trouble with the stroller in the elevator. They tended to be handsome, too, and always dressed in ways which she found, if not exactly impeccable, always interesting.

Allen and Douglas were her favorites. Douglas was tall and majestic-looking, with suspiciously bright blond hair. He often draped his coat over his shoulders, like a character from an American film of the forties. Allen was smaller, less precise in his appearance. He had fuzzy dark hair and seemed to be fond of bright colors; Milagros had seen him in scarlet earmuffs, purple mufflers, and once—when he had merely boarded the elevator to get his mail—in an oriental robe imprinted with the images of lime-green birds.

The conversation in the dining room was winding down. Mrs. Adler was making vague noises to show that she would consider the economical video surveillances, and Mrs. Sixth Floor was preparing to leave. Megan would be waking, cranking up to a fretful pitch, preparing to launch her incessant demands. From now until the hour their father returned, both girls would behave monstrously, but the moment they heard his key turn in the lock they would freeze in angelic attitudes.

Poor Mr. Adler would never realize that he lived in a household dominated by females, because Milagros made everything seem smooth and normal, greasing the way for him with her chocolate bribes and clandestine eavesdroppings. If he had asked her what she thought of his way of living, she could have replied, using the title of a movie she and Jewel had viewed on their day off: *Collision Course.*

"I'm practicing guerrilla warfare," Maryanne told Sarah when they met in the laundry room.

It was five days after the party in the lobby, and although Sarah went daily to the bookstore to keep track of the display case, the skeleton remained unchanged. He was still snorting coke into the cavernous nasal craters in his skull, and the crowd around the window had diminished. One more seven-day wonder.

"Aren't you interested?" Maryanne asked, shoveling garments into the washing machine with an almost vicious abandon. "Don't you want to know how I practice counterterrorism against the Yuppies?"

Sarah was caught off-guard. She had been noticing her own reflection, together with Maryanne's, in what appeared to be an expensive antique mirror. Someone had mounted the mirror directly in back of the washing machines, so that you had no choice but to look at yourself as you fed the machine's maw with fraying sheets and pungent knee socks and brassieres that looked grayish and sad under the fluorescent strip lighting. Maryanne looked shrewish in the unflattering light, but at least vivid and alive. Her olive skin was decidedly green, here in the basement, but her eyes and teeth flashed, black and white, respectively, within the green oval, whereas Sarah's pale face and fairish hair were blanched and formless. She looked like a mushroom. She supposed she had always looked like a mushroom in the laundry room, but never before had there been mirrors to bring the unpleasant fact to her attention.

"Sorry," she said, sprinkling a generic detergent over her load of washing. "Tell me how you go about counterterrorism."

Maryanne placed three quarters in her machine's slots and slammed them home. "Well," she said, "the only way to ruin a Yup's day is to make him, or her, suspect that the life he, or she, is leading—" She seemed to have lost her point somewhere in the jungles of gender, but rallied. ". . . is not worthwhile! Is not *enviable!*"

"And how do you put this point across?"

"Facial gestures, Sarah. You're walking along Columbus Avenue, right, trying to get to the deli to buy some toilet paper? You're hemmed in by all these humanoids in big coats, carrying little bags of salmon mousse or dill mustard from the Silver Palate shop. You pass that Cuban restaurant where they're all sitting in the window eating what looks like a plateful of mealworms mixed with melted tar. What do you do?"

"I can't imagine," said Sarah. "Avert your eyes?"

"No!" cried Maryanne, with what Sarah considered an exaggerated zeal. "You try to make eye contact, and then you look as if you want to throw up. You look at that plate of food and curl your lip, squeeze your eyes shut, and pinch your nostrils. I try to be as dramatic as I can."

"But what if they just think you're a madwoman?"

"Unlikely, but if they do, what does it matter? I've devalued their meal, ruined some of their pleasure."

Sarah laughed a little uneasily. Normally she would find this sort of thing amusing, and even sympathize, but Maryanne was too intense. "Another thing I've taken to doing is carrying a single-edged razor blade at all times, in my handbag."

"Not for protection, surely. A *razor* blade?"

"It's for those cars with burglar alarms that go off and nobody turns them off for hours? How can they go off so *often?* They must be special Yuppie alarms, set to react if you so much as walk too close to their cars." Maryanne opened her mouth and did a creditable imitation of the sort of wailing, irritable sirens they all heard so often.

"Here's what I do," she said, dancing quickly past the laundry table, her arm straight at her side, the imaginary razor blade slashing at the paint job of the imaginary car and then disappearing into her shoulder bag. "See? It's so simple, really, happens so fast nobody has a chance to see what I'm doing. I've only had two chances, so far, but you can bet they'll never park on *this* block again."

"But I would think Yuppies would use parking garages," said Sarah mildly.

"Oh, and another thing. In the supermarket I always make sure I have something overripe in my cart. A foul tomato, say, or a kiwi. An avocado would be ideal, but they're so rarely even ripe, let alone soft—"

"Please, Maryanne, I think you're getting too intense about this," said Sarah, but her friend seemed not to have heard.

"When those women with the really huge bags—what do they have in them, Krugerrands? Let me tell you, when you get sideswiped with one of those babies you feel like you're under attack! Once, I figure it could be an accident, but if it happens twice, accident or no accident, I lurch against them, crying out in pain, and squash that fruit all over their mink coat!"

Sarah giggled nervously, feeling relief that she was not alone in resenting the heavy and punishing bags. She wanted to say something reasonable and calming, but at that moment one of the au pair girls entered the laundry room, an infant strapped to her chest and a vast load of laundry wheeling in her wake. The moment was lost.

The bookstore window did not disappoint, after all. Just when everyone had given up on it as a source of neighborhood entertainment, the familiar skeleton vanished, along with his recreational drug of choice. Early one morning, a diligent Korean from the produce shop reported something unusual and disturbing. In the bookstore's display case there now reposed an object of vastly greater proportions. No skeleton this, but a lifelike body, crumpled in on itself and staring through the window like a mammoth fish confined in a ten-gallon tank. He seemed to

THREE

Some miracle of almost forgotten good taste prevented the networks from broadcasting the image of the man in the display case, and this was a great disappointment for those, like Milagros, who hadn't viewed him. Of the au pairs, only Jewel had been on the scene.

"You didn't want to see him, man," she told the others. "His face was just that gray"—she pointed to Teresa's leg warmers—"and his tongue was like *this.*" She allowed her own pink tongue to protrude slightly. "He was *nasty!*"

"His tongue was also gray?" asked Milagros.

Jewel shook her head ominously. Jeremy, the child she minded, was craning back in his stroller, listening.

"I'd say you'll be having the odd bad dream," said Teresa in her cheerful soprano. Three sets of dark eyes reproached her, and then the little band moved on, propelled by the cold, summoning their ambulatory charges and wheeling the others before them.

Milagros couldn't help wondering: if the man's head had really been shoved against the pane of glass, and if his tongue was hanging out, was it fair to say that the *muerto* was licking the window? She wanted to get it straight, in order to write an account of the murder to her mother. The *bruja* might be old-fashioned in some ways, but in matters of death she was always right on the mark.

The evening news teams featured heavily bundled reporters standing in front of the now-empty bookstore window, gabbling about unexpected death in the midst of ostentatious plenty.

"Police are not ruling out the notion that this murder could be drug-related," said one of them.

"The identity of the man in the bookstore window will not be released until his family has been notified," said another.

"This is a terrible tragedy," said Monica, who had been stopped by a roving reporter in the street. "I have lived in this neighborhood for a quarter of a century, and I can remember when we were considered a Target Crime Area. This should serve as an example to all who think we can afford to live in the illusionary."

She said a great deal more, but when her assembled guests gathered to watch the news, her utterances had been cropped. "This is a terrible tragedy," said the TV Monica. Period.

"I think," said Mrs. Strabinski, "we are once more a Target Crime Area."

Upstairs, Sarah Mason watched the news with a jaundiced eye. On the one hand, she didn't really care who the body in the display case might have been; on the other, she had a nagging feeling that she might have known him.

Mr. Crotty told anyone who would listen that the killer had to be someone with access to the bookstore—a former employee, a workman doing renovations, or the owner, and since this was so patently true he got no satisfying arguments. Even in the smallest hours of a wintry night, it would be impossible to hump a heavy corpse across the pavement and into the store without detection. *Somebody* was always about. Therefore, the unfortunate man had been murdered in the store and then shoved into his penultimate resting place.

Maryanne had a theory of her own, one she told only to Sarah. "I have a feeling, a very strong feeling, that it was What'shisname," she said, speaking in a low, conspiratorial voice over Sarah's telephone. "You know the one I mean—the guy who was always so helpful about Elizabeth."

"Elizabeth" was Elizabeth Jolley, their favorite novelist, whose books reached them, as if wafted on an unwholesome but delightful trade wind, from Australia. Sarah, who had been trying to type a transcript of an interview she'd done in London, sat back in her chair and tried to remember the name of the helpful young man who always ordered so promptly, but it was

no use. He had simply been a presence—thin, slightly effemi-
nate, wry, and efficient.

"Are you still there?" asked Maryanne.

"Of course I am. Why do you suspect him?"

"The whole caper is consistent with his sense of humor. Don't
you remember his calendar?"

Sarah remembered it well, especially since she had been in the
store when an angry member of the Animal Rights Movement
had picked a quarrel. The young man's calendar had been the
kind designed for writing in dates of important appointments,
and it had hung on the wall back near the Penguin Paperbacks.
He had inked in fanciful and tongue-in-cheek appointments
with destiny, like *Tamper with Tylenol at Pathmark Drugs* or *Spray-
paint Sushi Bar.* The one that had irked the animal activist read
Torture Kittens. Sarah saw that he and Maryanne were, in some
sense, soul mates.

"I remember," she said. "But just because he had a bizarre
sense of humor, well, that doesn't mean he was capable of killing, does it?"

A long sigh came down the phone. "As the store's former
manager, he probably had a key. Access. Opportunity. As someone who'd been put out of a job, he had motive."

"To kill indiscriminately, Maryanne?"

"Who said it was indiscriminate, dear? I'll bet you anything
that fat stiff turns out to be the landlord. He even *looked* like a
landlord. A dead one."

"But what would make a landlord and a store manager con-
verge in the middle of the night at a place that's already been
sold?"

"Destiny," said Maryanne, laughing now. "That's what. I just
hope he gets away with it, too! Hooray for What'shisname!"

As it happened, Maryanne was right about the victim. Solemn
news teams informed their listeners of the identity of the man in
the display case. He was Leonard Norbert Muellen, aged sixty-
two, and he had, indeed, been the landlord of the property in
question, a property whose value had increased tenfold between

the time it had been acquired and the time when the bookstore lost its lease.

Mr. Muellen had no immediate family. The manager of the defunct bookstore, a Mr. Gordon Childs, was being sought for questioning. Any persons knowing of Mr. Childs' whereabouts were ardently invited to call a special police number, with anonymity guaranteed.

Further details would be forthcoming when the coroner felt capable of issuing a full report.

Milagros liked, sometimes, to have a chat with the building's super, Ernesto, even though she felt vaguely superior to him. Ernesto was a Puerto Rican of middling years who seemed completely content to service the building, as he had done for years before it became a co-op, without ever seeming to think of advancement. Ernesto wanted only to work until his retirement, and then move back to Cabo Rojo with his union pension and enjoy his remaining years.

This seemed a bleak prospect to Milagros, who had much more daring plans. She saw a future in which she would pursue her goal to become a fashion designer, aided by the comfortable funds of a well-off American husband. They would live on Central Park West, and once she had become established in her own right, she would bring her mother to New York and set her up in a nice apartment—preferably not too close—and feel both virtuous and unbelievably lucky at the same time. Her stepfather would definitely have to remain behind, in Honduras, where he would regret his awful behavior to Milagros until the day he died.

On the day after the identity of the corpse had been revealed, Milagros encountered Ernesto on the pavement in front of the building. He was stacking plastic sacks of garbage near the service entrance. She was without Phoebe and Megan for once, because the little girls had the sniffles and Mrs. Adler had sent her to the supermarket with a silly list. Gringo-ish items like yogurt and Worcestershire sauce were apparently needed, not to mention endive and winter squash. What made the list truly insufferable was Mrs. Adler's insistence that some of the purchases might be made at Food World, while others should be bought at the Korean vegetable store a whole block away, on Broadway. Milagros wondered if Mrs. Adler could be fooled. Would she know the difference between a winter squash from Food World and one from the Koreans?

She decided to bring it up, speaking to Ernesto. Today they spoke in English, as Milagros had once half-heartedly requested, in an effort to improve her skills.

"You better do like she says," said Ernesto. "That one has the eye like a hawk. Maybe she going to ask you for the sales slip, to prove."

"That would be crazy, señor."

"Nooooo," said Ernesto. He spoke with the sternness of one who felt the need to protect his employers. "Mrs. Adler, she's a nice lady. Not crazy."

Milagros walked off haughtily, without a backward look. Ernesto's last words, spoken this time in Spanish, reached her grateful ears as she was about to approach Columbus Avenue.

The crazy one is Señor Crotty, cried Ernesto passionately. *Believe me—I know!*

Once inside Food World, Milagros permitted herself to mull over the super's remark. Old Crotty had never seemed particularly crazy to her. Boring, perhaps, but not crazy. Slowly she pushed her cart toward the dairy section. Innumerable tiny old ladies impeded her progress, wheeling their carts down the center of the isle at a snail's pace, or stopping suddenly, craning upward at items far beyond their reach. Since Milagros was almost as small as they, she was never asked to help, but Jewel had told her how the old ones were forever securing her aid. "You're nice and tall, dear, would you mind?" was what they said, and Jewel always helped. Milagros felt irritation for the old ladies, because they made her feel pity, and because if she lived long enough she might find herself in the same plight.

Finally she made her way to the shelves of yogurt and began her selection for Mrs. Adler. The Adlers were certainly not crazy, nor were the people Jewel and Noreen worked for, as far as she knew. Teresa's people were borderline, though. Mrs. Spooner had skittering eyes and talked to herself, according to

Teresa. The quaint one who had visited Mrs. Adler could *seem* crazy, babbling about Target Crime Areas, but Milagros sensed no evil from her.

She was becoming interested in her catalogue of lunacy, so interested that she didn't really mind the bottleneck which prevented her from wheeling into the aisle where the Worcestershire sauce lived. A handsome black stock clerk was trying to catch her eye, making fluid motions with his hands and rolling his own eyes comically as if to invite her to join in his merriment at the chaos of Food World, but Milagros refused to acknowledge him.

Who else could be crazy in the building? The Anglo writer who pecked away at her typewriter above the nanny room seemed sane enough, even if she appeared to be haggard and preoccupied at times in the elevator. Whenever they met, at the door or in the laundry room, the writer was friendly and cheerful. All in all, there was only one person in the building who inspired uneasy feelings in Milagros, and that was the tall, rapier-thin man with the neat little beard who lived in the penthouse. His name was wonderful, the name of an American hero if ever she had heard one—Barnett Seawright! And the sea was there, in his eyes. They were the palest green, so pale, in fact, that they did not in the least resemble any saltwater she had ever seen; if Mr. Seawright made her think of an ocean, it was more like that of the Arctic regions, icy and inhospitable. Or perhaps—Milagros smiled to herself, for she had been a very good student of geography—the Antarctic was more like it. Just as no one really lived in Antarctica, except for a few visiting scientists who studied penguins, no one seemed to be at home behind Barnett Seawright's chilly eyes. He smiled with his lips and big, perfect, teeth, but the eyes did not participate.

Milagros homed in on the condiments department at last, squirming as she recalled her one direct confrontation with the man in question. She had seen him in the elevator, of course, but he had not seemed to see her. Unlike the others, he never smiled at Megan or Phoebe, and he left the elevator the moment it descended to the lobby, without a backward look. She hadn't known, in the early days, that he lived in the penthouse, and she was still ignorant of the fact on the ill-fated day she decided to make a pilgrimage to the roof.

It had been her day off, and she and Jewel had arranged to go to a movie in the multiplex cinema uptown. With time to spare, Milagros had taken the elevator to the ninth floor and mounted the little staircase to the roof. Here she found a corridor painted in soothing cream shades. Three doors challenged her. One was clearly the door to the occupied penthouse, another the door to the other penthouse, whose owner was away. The third bore a legend which read Fire Door, and it had been this one she pushed open and walked through. At first she had seen only grayish tiles and then, rounding a corner, Mother of Christ! What a view! She could see far and away, from this vantage point, to Central Park on the one side and the river to the west. She could see the greenish attics of the Dakota, where John Lennon had been murdered, and the seamy rooftop of the squalid building directly opposite—the last holdout in the neighborhood—where the ambulances so regularly called to remove the bodies of persons Milagros associated with Home.

Enchanted, she had crept over a sort of parapet, and that had been her biggest mistake. She was in a sort of jungle—again reminding her of Honduras—peculiarly populated with little tables that had beach umbrellas sheltering them. Two women in bikini bathing suits sat beneath one umbrella, drinking from tall glasses and looking agitated and bored at the same time. One of them looked up and grinned, and Milagros had begun to back away, sensing that she did not belong in this picture—not yet—when a cruel hand had encircled her upper arm, pressing painfully. It had been the hand of Barnett Seawright, dressed in shorts and a loose T-shirt. *Who was she? What was she doing on his roof? Did she know she was trespassing on private property? Was she aware that he owned the exclusive rights to the roof garden? Didn't she realize, under the terms of the Proprietary Lease, that he, a legal shareholder, was the only one entitled to enjoy the roof? Did she want him to call the police, or was it merely a matter to be taken up at the next meeting of the Board of Directors?*

Milagros edged her way into the checkout line, remembering the terror Mr. Seawright had inspired in her on that balmy day, and hating him for the impersonal way in which he had frightened her, looking through her as if she had no more substance than a homeless nuisance encountered, begging, at the subway's entrance.

It didn't improve her mood at all to remember that Barnett Seawright, the craziest of all those who lived in her new building, was the President of the Board of Directors.

FOUR

"Miss Mason? Miss Sarah Mason, or should I say *Ms?*" The voice was oddly muffled, as if the speaker were standing a foot from the phone, and it was also a familiar voice, but Sarah could not really place it. It was half past one in the morning, and she had been ready to go to bed.

"Yes," she said. "Who's this?"

"It's Gordon Childs."

Gordon Childs? Did she know a Gordon Childs? Certainly not well enough to have him phone her at such an intimate time.

"From the bookstore," he said. "You know. The *book*store."

Sarah felt a little prickle of recognition. This was the voice of the reedy clerk, the helpful one Maryanne called What'shisname, but it was devoid of its usual tone of self-congratulatory irony. Gordon Childs sounded terrified. "Where are you, Gordon?" she asked.

"Oh, no, oh no you don't," he said. "I can't trust anyone, can I? I can't possibly tell you where I am."

"This isn't a confession, is it, Gordon?" Her tape recorder was in another room, and she pawed at her bedside table, reaching for a piece of legal-sized paper she'd placed under a coffee cup to keep from making rings.

"No!" cried Gordon Childs, sounding really anguished now. "I haven't done anything, Sarah. May I call you Sarah? Well, I may have done *something*, but certainly not—you know. Not *that.*"

"How did you get my number?"

A pause. "The truth?" Gordon Childs asked rhetorically, seeming to suppress an ill-advised chuckle. "If I tell you the truth, then maybe you'll trust me. It puts me in a bad light, you see, and I wouldn't do that unless I were being unconditionally frank and candid with you. Don't you agree?"

"I'm not sure. Try me."

"It would be so simple for me to lie and say I had your number from the customer list, even though we don't have phone numbers for preferred customers, only addresses for the mailing list, but you wouldn't be likely to notice, would you?"

"My number is unlisted," said Sarah.

"Exactly. But I have it because whenever you used a charge card you had to write it on the slip—Visa, wasn't it?"

Sarah had an unpleasant vision of the clerk lovingly saving the carbons from her Visa transactions. Perhaps he was obsessed with her, based on what he perceived to be her superior literary tastes, tastes which coincided with his own?

"The thing is," said Gordon Childs, "I used to copy down the, ah, pertinent information on credit card slips. I have it all in a little tablet. I won't lie to you, Sarah; I thought it might come in handy if I ever planned to turn my hand to a life of crime." He spoke the last three words as if in inverted commas, a reversion to his old, ironic style. "But—and this is important, Sarah—I decided a long time ago that I would never use you or your friend, Mrs. Francini, or five or six others. That was a decision I made way before the old carbon scam was exposed."

"And what do we privileged few have to thank for being on the exempt list?" asked Sarah, feeling cross and intrigued at the same time.

"Time is running out, and we haven't addressed the important issues, but here goes. Morally, I would feel that I was violating my own code of ethics if I made use of your credit card. You are a discriminating reader. You and the other exempts made me feel that I was doing something of value. Surely you understand?"

"What about the others?" Sarah uncapped a pen and prepared to jot down Gordon's response against her cocked-up knees. "What about the ones who bought books only from the Best-Seller Section? What about the students who had to buy Flannery O'Connor just because she was on the syllabus?"

"They usually paid in cash."

"What about the idiots who bought their weight in gold in self-help books? You carried quite a lot of them for a while, on that table in the rear."

"They would have been the first to be used," agreed Gordon, "but it never came to that."

"I suppose that's something to be grateful for. Why did you say time was running out? Surely you can't think my phone is tapped? Nobody would connect us."

"It's that I don't have another quarter. Don't say you'll call me back, because I'm not entirely stupid, you know. I don't want anyone tracing this number."

"I never believed you killed that man, anyway. Mrs. Francini does, incidentally, but she hopes you get away with it. But pulling a disappearing act! Why do something that makes you look so guilty?"

"Because I *am* guilty," said Gordon impatiently. "Probably it's more than a misdemeanor, but it's less than a felony. The police might not believe me, though."

Sarah sighed and wished she had a cigarette, but they, too, were in the other room. It was one of her methods of cutting down—leaving the cigarettes far from the places she tended to smoke most, the typewriter and the telephone.

"Why have you called, Gordon? What is it I can do for you?"

And then, far too soon, it seemed, a tiresome computerized voice cut in on the line, demanding more money. In the little time he had left, Gordon desperately tried to get his message across. Sarah was to contact the precinct house and ask the detectives on the bookstore case how serious a crime it was to—something about moving. A moving violation? Removing evidence? She was sure he would call again when he'd obtained another quarter, but though she read in bed until three o'clock, the phone was silent.

The monthly meeting of the Board of Directors took place three days after the identity of the murdered man had been revealed. These meetings were held in a solemn conference room in the offices of the building's Managing Agent, the Perchley Company. They were open to any shareholder who cared to attend, and in the co-op's earliest days there had been quite a gathering. Mr. Crotty had been a regular, the manila envelope under his arm bristling with memoranda containing useful suggestions, and the usual petitioners had made their way to Fifth Avenue, eager to present plans for renovation or air grievances about water damage, loud stereos, barking dogs, or obstreperous children thundering overhead. They had all come, as first-time jurors do, to experience democracy in action, to participate in the cooperative process, and to see that justice was done.

The killing dullness of the meetings had swiftly eradicated all but the diehards. Mr. Crotty had hung in for nearly a year before withdrawing. The meetings were not merely boring, they were excruciatingly so, as if the Inquisition had been reconstituted in twentieth-century Manhattan and emerged with such a sophisticated method of torture that even the most determined combatants preferred to live with their problems rather than submit them to arbitration. The conference room was overheated, producing a lethargy so pervasive that even nonsmokers begged cigarettes in order to convince themselves that they were still alive.

Twenty minutes of discussion about the building's fickle boiler could seem to last for a week. By the time the printed agenda indicated attention must be paid to the elevator, even the hardiest could read beyond and note that Fire Doors and Laundry Room and Storage Space and Bids for Roof Repair must be addressed before they could hope to speak.

The second Board, headed by Barnett Seawright, had changed all that. Shareholders' complaints, provided they were introduced by the Board's secretary in a written note, were tackled first. By that time, most of the shareholders had given up. To be present at a Board Meeting, the conventional wisdom went, was to ruin a whole week of one's life. The days that went before the meeting were spent in dread; the days following were spent in the sad acknowledgment that one had been a fool to show up in the first place.

In late January, Monica was the only member of the Board who entered the airless conference room with a feeling of cheer. She loved the sound of her own voice, and the prospect of reading several letters of complaint into the minutes filled her with a bracing sense of purposefulness. She had rehearsed the manner in which she would read Mrs. Adler's correspondence, which had to do with the way in which Mrs. Adler's sink mysteriously overflowed whenever the homosexuals upstairs used their state-of-the-art dishwasher.

Imagine Monica's distress when the main topic of discussion proved to be the possible roof damage brought about by Mr. Seawright's jungle? Barnett had brought a detailed engineer's report which proved that his plants were not exerting enough pressure on any square foot of the existing roof to cause the damage so amply recorded on the top floor. Barnett was passionate in the defense of his roof plantation, and Monica never had a chance to make her well-rehearsed speech, because the agenda indicated that the next item under consideration involved a prospective buyer.

Applications for ownership were always tricky. The first Board had welcomed the opportunity to screen potential new neighbors, although one of the ousted members—Seawright had made an almost-clean sweep when it was time for new elections —had complained that she didn't feel it quite right to examine the tax returns and financial statements of complete strangers. Monica remembered it well, as the only carryover from those early times, the only one to win her seat on the Board back when Barnett Seawright spoke of clean slates and carried the day. She hated to think what might happen if anyone voiced such a quaint concern now!

It was *all* money now. Seawright had explained how the only thing that mattered was the applicant's financial statement, and if it wasn't up to snuff, then they were to turn the person down without any explanation. The word "assets" was often used, but not in the old way, when Monica might study an information packet and pronounce: "I think this couple sounds like they would be an ambience in our community—they would be assets."

"What other assets?" asked Ed Knowles, bending intimately across the table in Barnett Seawright's direction, interrupting Monica's reverie.

They were pawing through an information packet on a couple called Burgess. Mr. Burgess earned a salary of $85,000 a year, and owned a country property in upstate New York valued at $150,000. Mr. and Mrs. Burgess had only $21,000 in their savings account, but they were only thirty-five and thirty-one, respectively. Mrs. Burgess did not work, but she listed as an asset rare books evaluated at $17,000 and, far more importantly for Monica, who had an abiding interest in the arts, there was a character reference appended to Mrs. Burgess's file that indicated that she was a member in good standing of Alternative Voices, a group which encouraged the literary efforts of newcomers from the Third World. The Burgesses planned to take out a loan to pay for their apartment, and Monica thought they'd be easily able to swing it, what with Mr. Burgess' salary and his wife's outgoing nature, which was bound to add to their coffers. Her arm was cocked, ready to vote "aye," when Barnett Seawright's persuasive voice summed the situation up.

"These people can't reasonably be expected to live up to their obligations," he said. "My feeling is that we should reject them out of hand. Their application is an insult."

Monica's hand flew up and received the magisterial nod. "Why is it ridiculous?" she asked. "Mr. Burgess earns a good salary, doesn't he? In my prime, eighty-five thousand dollars a year was a king's ransom."

"Marvelous," muttered Ed Knowles, shaking his head in amusement.

"You see, Monica," said Seawright, "we can't afford to revert to outmoded standards. What would happen to the corporation if Mr. Burgess dies and Louise Burgess were compelled to carry on? She has no known means of support, and extremely meager assets."

He was smiling at her with barely repressed irritation, as if she couldn't distinguish between a real smile and the simple baring of teeth, and this only put Monica in a combative frame of mind. "This building was never intended for millionaires," she said. "And when you make reference to no known means of support for Mrs. Burgess, you are speaking wrongly. She is married to her spouse, and that is her means of support, and since he earns a good salary and in the course of events will probably earn more and isn't likely to die—not at thirty-five—" Monica drew breath. "I think I'll vote for him," she concluded.

"You're not *voting* for him, dear," said the managing agent, looking about twelve, who sat at the other end of the table. "This isn't a popularity contest. I'm sure the Burgesses are pleasant people, but I agree with Barnett."

"Well, couldn't we at least meet them?" Monica smiled, to show how reasonable her request was, but Seawright shot forward in his chair as if she had proposed something shocking.

"No!" he said. "No, Monica. The one thing a board must never do is meet with applicants they are planning to reject. We are well within our rights, I repeat, *well* within our rights, to reject them solely on financial reasons."

In the end, Monica voted with them, making it unanimous. She had thought she would be the holdout, so she could say "Let the record show, etcetera," but what was the point? She quickly adjusted to a new view of herself, that of a humanitarian liberal whose natural generosity had to be curbed for its own good. It never occurred to her to wonder why she, alone of the earlier Board, had met with no opposition from Seawright when the elections had been held. She thought it was because she was popular.

"We may not always concur together," she told Barnett as they filed out of the conference room, "but you have exquisite taste. Your Bunberry coat is absolutely gorgeous."

"Thank you, dear," said the President of the Board of Directors, smiling, for the first time to Monica's knowledge, with a degree of real mirth.

Long past the hour when the Board members were asleep, and even beyond the time when Sarah Mason had given up on another call from Gordon Childs, Mr. Crotty was sacking his garbage. Pickup times were at eight in the morning and four in the afternoon, and fines were threatened if shareholders ignored the rules. Garbage had to be securely contained in large plastic bags, and it must not make its appearance too early or too late.

Mr. Crotty appreciated the wisdom of these directives. Reeking garbage, especially in the summer months, lounging near the service elevator, would give a slummy air to the building. Guests who arrived for a dinner party at a C- or D-line apartment should not be subjected to the fumes of rotting melons or rancid yogurt cartons. He sealed his plastic bag, twisting it round with vigor in one hand and throttling its neck with a stay-lock binding.

His retirement and solitary state, now that Kitty was dead, had thrust him into a new life he had never anticipated. His son owned the apartment where he had been born, and Mr. Crotty was merely a kind of caretaker. His new, flexible hours both confused and occasionally delighted him. He could stay up half the night, and sleep until he woke up! Usually, Mr. Crotty woke between six and seven-thirty in the morning, but on several occasions he had daringly awakened at new and exotic hours. Why should he be obliged to set his alarm in order to make sure his garbage was deposited by 8:00 A.M.?

Similarly, why should he feel constrained to return to the apartment before four in the afternoon, if he happened to find himself in congenial conversation in Central Park or O'Reilly's Pub at about that hour? The wee hours were the answer, right enough. Lug the rubbish out at four in the morning, and who was to know? Sack it well and place it near the service elevator just before dawn, and who could say it hadn't been dropped there at a quarter to eight?

Well-pleased with his stratagem, Mr. Crotty unlatched his many locks and hauled his garbage to its resting place. On the return trip, he saw that the fire doors were slightly ajar. The central staircase within the building had been constructed to ensure that the north-facing tenants—those not blessed with fire escapes—could flee to safety in the event of a conflagration.

Mr. Crotty was in the act of pushing the fire doors shut when he saw something he did not wish to see. A long, thin figure, clad in dark clothing and crowned with a skullcap of black wool, appeared to be loitering in the gloom of the fire stairs. Mr. Crotty's scrutiny of the figure seemed inconsequential. He continued to stand, head bowed, arms stiffly at his side, on the top stair of Mr. Crotty's landing.

He seemed so much a classic apparition that Mr. Crotty sped back to his own apartment, not sure that he had seen the ominous figure. Logic told him that he had, but Mr. Crotty had once again drunk more whiskey than was good for him and feared that he might be hallucinating, or whatever it was the young folks called it.

FIVE

Sarah took Maryanne into her confidence about the phone call from the bookstore clerk. They could agree on one thing only, and that was the fact that Gordon Childs must still be in the area, if he had used his last quarter to make the call.

"I see it like this," said Maryanne, who was trying to iron a blouse on her breadboard and finding it difficult. "Gordon had a key to the store, and he came back for some reason. Maybe he wanted to make sure he'd left nothing behind, maybe he'd lost his place to live and used the store as a squat at night. Anyway, he finds the landlord already murdered and goes flittering around in a panic, wondering what to do. He doesn't want to get involved with the police, but he *does* want to know who the dead man is."

"Surely he'd know?"

"Not necessarily. How many employees ever see their landlord? But he would know his name. So he removed the guy's wallet, carefully wiping off any fingerprints, and looked at his driver's license. Then, after confirming that the corpse is indeed the bloodsucking Muellen, he notices a fat wad of bills. He is desperate for cash, and the man won't need it anymore, so Gordon removes the money and skedaddles."

"You're forgetting something," said Sarah, vaguely wondering what had happened to Maryanne's ironing board. "He would have seen the corpse in the window from the street. He would never have gone in, under the circumstances. He'd have removed himself as far from the scene of the crime as possible."

"Not necessarily. He might not have even looked at the window. When you've gone to a specific place hundreds of times, you don't bother to look. You have your key ready, you stick it in the lock, *voilà*. I grant you he would have had to do something complicated with the riot gates, but if he'd been doing it by rote for several years? It was bitterly cold, no one on the street at that late hour, right? He might have been inside the store for an hour before something made him notice the thing in the window."

"But if he'd taken money and wiped away any fingerprints, why bother to be afraid of this so-called crime he's guilty of? The police wouldn't know."

"Guilt," said Maryanne. "He probably had a Catholic upbringing, like me."

"I don't think Gordon Childs suffers much from your classical guilt pattern, Maryanne. He was quite breezy when he told me about the carbon scam."

Maryanne whirled about, grinning. "And wasn't I quite breezy when I told you about my war on Yuppies? Make no mistake, sweetie, I expect—well, a part of me expects—to burn in hell for slashing Yup-mobiles and trashing expensive furs. But I go on doing it, don't I?"

"I guess you do," said Sarah impartially. She did not want to add that Maryanne's acts of counterterrorism reminded her of the Luddites, while Gordon's seemed more modern, more fired by the notion of conceptual art. Maryanne, after all, was supposed to be the expert on visuals, while Sarah was concerned with words and language.

"You guess I do?" Maryanne's voice had risen. "Only today, not two hours ago, I had a little episode in Food World. I knocked some cranapple juice off a shelf and ruined a pair of suede boots. They belonged to this bimbo in a fox coat who was actually reading *People* magazine in the center of the aisle, translating the good bits to her Significant Other. They were Eurotrash, Sarah, and they wouldn't let me by. They were parked in the middle of the aisle, gabbling about Princess Caroline of Monaco, and I was only trying to wheel my cart to the V-8s and make a speedy getaway."

"I think you make these things up," Sarah said. "By the way, what happened to your ironing board?"

"I never owned one. I refused to iron Bill's shirts when we were married, so it doesn't seem fair to reverse the rule for myself."

"But you *are* ironing your shirt."

"Too expensive to send it out, the way I did Bill's. Reduced circumstances, and all that. But buying an ironing board would be going too far."

"Hmmm." Sarah understood, in a way, because of her own ex-husband's intense irritation about the defrosting of the refrigerator. She had always waited until the small freezer compartment looked like an igloo, and defrosting became a major project involving her hair dryer and many newspapers. Mark always had to help, sometimes going at the thing with his claw hammer. Now that he was gone, she resisted impulses to defrost at a reasonable time and always waited until the igloo appeared. She supposed it was a sort of loyalty, a kind of counterproductive code of ethics she seemed to share with Maryanne. On the order of, if not the same, as Gordon's decision not to rip off customers who read good books.

"I think you're wrong about Gordon," she told Maryanne. "If Gordon's in hiding, he has a very good reason. I think he knows who did kill Muellen, and removed evidence to protect the killer."

"And the killer was the one putting skeletons and fake coke in the window? Come on, Sarah. That was so definitely the kind of statement Gordon would make! Like his calendar—why are you laughing?"

"Because you're absolutely right. Gordon found the murdered man somewhere in the bookstore, and he couldn't resist making his last great visual statement. It was the *pièce de résistance* of his window displaying, and so very appropriate. A chance like that doesn't come along more than once in a lifetime."

Maryanne turned from the breadboard, eyes flashing. "Bingo," she said. "You're on to something. Is there anything we should do? The police, do you think?"

"No," said Sarah. "I don't think we can do anything now. Just wait and see what happens."

The search for Gordon Childs was shaping up as a manhunt for a dangerous criminal. The network news teams ran breathless profiles on the wanted man. A photograph of Gordon always accompanied the profiles, and it was always the same one —a snapshot taken two years earlier, when the suspect had been twenty-five. Gordon was shown at his manager's desk in the bookstore, pretending to set fire to a Harold Robbins best-seller. He was leering comically, and looked quite insane.

He had lived in Queens with his mother until quite recently, when her death, while on vacation in Florida, bequeathed the house in Astoria to a sister, who had sold it and turned Gordon out. The sister, a Mrs. Phyllis Pugh, would say only that she had not seen Gordon for three years and that was fine with her. He had always been a strange boy. Two other employees of the bookstore affirmed Mrs. Pugh's opinion of Gordon, although one, a bespectacled woman who wore her glasses on a stout chain, sturdily said that Gordon's eccentricities did not mean that he was capable of murder.

There was no known address for him in New York City, and nothing connected him to the sudden death of his mother, who had perished in Miami when she crossed a street against the light. Gordon had been working at the bookstore when his mother died. He had no previous criminal record. He did have the sister, who lived in Hartford, but she proved to be equally unhelpful. She had not seen Gordon for years, and the age difference was such that they had never been close. Gordon had been born in his mother's middle age, just three years before his father's death. He had been, it seemed, the classic "surprise."

The one person who could be said to have the strongest motive for killing Mr. Muellen, the store's owner, was firmly beyond any trace of suspicion, at least in terms of having performed the act himself. At the time of the Bookstore Atrocity, he had been in Roosevelt Hospital, preparing to undergo a gallbladder operation. He declined to be interviewed from his hospital bed, but sent the following message to reporters: *Let me quell any suggestion that I might have hired someone to kill the individual who died in my late bookstore. Thanks to Mr. Muellen, I am bankrupt and could not possibly afford to hire a taxi, much less a hit man.*

All in all, Gordon Childs seemed the best bet. He went from "missing store manager" or "runaway clerk" to "Fugitive Gordon Childs" before the coroner had issued his report.

Fortunately for Megan and Phoebe, they were not with Milagros when she went, humming, into the laundry room near the end of that hectic week. New washers and dryers had recently been installed, and the room had been painted with a cheerful coat of new white latex, but Milagros felt nervous and lonely whenever she entered the basement room after dark. It was only seven at night, but the early dark outside and the lurid light inside gave her a creepy, disoriented feeling, which is why she was humming. Always, when Mrs. Adler sent her to the laundry room near the cutoff time, Milagros experienced dread. What if the elevator, which discontinued service to the basement after seven-thirty, malfunctioned and she were forced to spend all the night in the bowels of the building? She had checked once, and there was no way back to the safer world above. The garbage exit was padlocked, the escapes to the courtyard were barred by steel fire doors, and all around her lay a labyrinth of shadowy tunnels leading to dead ends.

It would be like a story she had once read, in which a man plunged over a cliff only to land on a little outcropping of rock, cushioned with moss, where he had to spend the night. His life had been spared, but the horror of the long night—the sea lashing beneath him and the screams of the gulls—had deprived him of his sanity. When the rescue team brought him up the following day, the man's hair had turned completely white. That was what a night in the laundry room would do to her, probably.

She was standing at the folding table, sorting out the small dungarees and washable tops of Phoebe and Megan, when the full horror of Señor Crotty's peculiar inquiries took hold of her. Riding down on the elevator, she had felt the machine grind to a halt before it had even reached the lobby. The doors had slid open and Señor Crotty, with an apologetic air, had thrust his head inside.

"Just making a spot check," he had rumbled. "Seen anyone suspicious on the premises, miss?"

She trembled a little as she remembered how she had humored the old man, pretending to consider for his sake, and then shaking her head. No, not a soul. But what if he knew something she did not? Even now a mad rapist might be hiding in the shadows of the laundry room, waiting to pounce at the moment of cutoff time! And then she recalled what Ernesto had said, that the only crazy one was, in fact, Señor Crotty.

Milagros swept the unfolded garments into the laundry cart, avoiding the row of manacled bicycles hovering in the gloomiest corner of the room, and wheeled off toward the comparative safety of the elevator. She had almost reached the door when she had to pass two elderly refrigerators parked along the south wall. They were the rejected refrigerators of the new people, who had their kitchens renovated, and they seemed lonely to her. Tall, narrow, and cream in color, they had the misfortune of containing only one small freezer compartment. The new people required larger freezers, and devices which produced ice at regular intervals.

Milagros paused briefly to lay one hand against the shell of an outmoded giant—a gesture of condolence—and noticed that it was full. It seemed to be crammed with discarded clothing. Milagros could distinguish what looked like a balled-up blue shirt, and down where the veg crisper should be she saw some soft leather shoes with little tassels. Someone—the donor of all these good clothes to charity, perhaps—must have removed the shelves of the refrigerator in order to cram in so much.

There was even a flat disk of a golden watch strapped to what appeared to be a wrist, now that she dared to examine the strange collection more closely. She thought crazily of a scarecrow, decked out so splendidly and then shoved any which way into this tall box in the basement. It didn't make any sense.

Very slowly, she allowed her eyes to ascend to the uppermost regions, where the little freezer box would have been, and saw something which caused her to drop the laundry cart and run for the elevator. She stabbed at the button again and again, as if her violent motions could cause the machine to hurry, and when it arrived she scuttled into the elevator cab, hunkering down in a corner and gnawing at her fist. Somewhere between the third and fourth floors she began to scream, and by the time she had reached the Adlers' floor she was weeping uncontrollably. Mr.

Adler had to physically pry her from the cab, while doors opened and neighbors' heads shot out inquiringly.

Not until she had sobbed and shrieked in his comforting arms for a full five minutes did Milagros part with the truth. It seemed that the green eyes which had so frightened and insulted her on the penthouse terrace had pursued her to the laundry room.

"Robin Hood Killer Stalks Columbus Avenue" howled the *Post* in its morning edition the next day. The financially insecure among the shareholders pondered the wisdom of the headline. The historical Robin Hood had robbed the rich to give to the poor. Certainly the bookstore landlord and Barnett Seawright, President of the Board of Directors, had been rich, and equally certainly they had been deprived of their lives, but how would their deaths benefit the poor?

What was in it for *them?*

Mr. Crotty, quivering with a sense of obligation, wrote a long speech to be delivered at the emergency meeting in the lobby. He was torn by the twin impulses of duty and enlightenment. He would be called upon to describe the shadowy figure in the stairwell, and to explain why he had not acted with more alacrity. It would be like old times!

SIX

The detectives who now became a familiar sight in the building were called Dumbrowski and Fields, respectively. Dumbrowski was a dumpling of a man, if a dumpling could be hard and compact, with innocent-looking blue eyes and rapidly disappearing, baby-fine fair hair. His partner was a black man with a finely planed face and liquid eyes which gave the impression of never blinking. Dumbrowski, at thirty-six, looked ten years older, while Fields, who appeared scarcely out of his teens to the older shareholders, was in fact thirty-two.

They questioned all of the shareholders, floor by floor, apartment by apartment, always asking the same questions. When was the last time Monica, or Sarah, or Mrs. Strabinski, had seen Mr. Seawright? Had they noticed anything unusual? Had they visited the laundry room on the day the au pair made her discovery? Had they observed any strangers in the building? Had Mr. Seawright had any special contact with the bookstore where the earlier crime had taken place? Did they know of anyone who might harbor a grudge against the deceased?

Some of the respondents to these questions were terse and not very helpful, while others treated the arrival of the detectives as a social occasion of the jolliest kind, even if they themselves did not know how much the murder had perked them up. A few showed fear and wanted to know what the police would do for them in the way of security, but only two revealed anything of importance.

Teresa Blaney, a native of County Westmeath, Ireland, who was employed by a family called Spooner, was prepared to swear that she had been in the laundry room at 4:30 P.M. on the fateful day. She had noticed nothing unusual. To say that she had not purposely peered into the fridge was not to qualify her judgment because, she explained, she could hardly be in a room with a dead man without knowing it.

More exciting was a Mr. Crotty's statement about a dark figure lurking in the well of the fire stairs on the night before the murder. Unfortunately, Mr. Crotty couldn't describe the intruder other than to say he had been dressed in dark clothing, and when he was asked why he had not phoned the police, the old gentleman said the hour had been late and he had been sleepy and, on reflection, had doubted what he had seen. In light of the recent, tragic event, Mr. Crotty bitterly regretted his passivity. He volunteered to man what he called a "stakeout," to aid the police, an operation in which he would regularly check the fire stairs during the small hours of the night and report his findings with a walkie-talkie directly to a strategically placed patrol car, and seemed disappointed when his offer was ignored.

The laundry room became a Crime Scene and was sealed off to all but the police, as was Barnett Seawright's penthouse apartment. The fire stairs were searched diligently, but whatever was found there remained a secret to the neighbors of the dead man.

Privately, Dumbrowski and Fields mulled over one single, interesting fact. If there was a dearth of information on Barnett Seawright, it was because he appeared to be a man neither loved nor hated. The surviving members of the Board of Directors had obviously agreed to present a united front, and characterized him as a rather remote but fair-minded man, one whose attitude could seem chilly at first, but who had put in many long hours for the good of the building.

Those who had been nervous, or even tearful, were not mourning the loss of the actual man—they were afraid because they now lived in a building whose titular leader had been stabbed in the back and then crammed unceremoniously into an abandoned refrigerator in the basement.

The Honduran girl who had discovered the body could count herself lucky that the blood from Seawright's body had been invisible to her. Nearly all of it had been absorbed in the yards of cotton which had gone into the making of his fashionably baggy pants. The pants, labeled CHUMPS FOR CHAMPS, had been purchased at a popular boutique near the fatal bookstore.

For his own amusement, Roland Fields had calculated the yardage of the bloodstained trousers and come up with a figure indicating that Barnett Seawright's pants might have clothed three medium-sized women in Haiti, the country where his mother had been born.

Once more, as in the old, heady days before they had become a cooperative, the tenants found themselves packed into the lobby. Most had brought their own folding chairs. A few sat on the narrow marble ledge beneath the mailboxes, and the overflow squatted on the stairs leading to the second floor. Monica had requisitioned one of the deep leather chairs that had appeared in the lobby soon after the conversion; Allen Moorehead, of Allen and Douglas, lounged in the other, wearing an orange bathrobe and a surgical mask.

"I've had the most awful flu," he told newcomers as they stepped from the elevator, "and I do believe in keeping a bad thing to myself. Douglas is in Philadelphia on business, but I promised him I'd take notes tonight. He doesn't want to miss a thing."

Someone on the staircase had lit a cigarette, and Monica began to flap her hands.

"Have a heart," called Maryanne Francini from her canvas stool. "People get nervous when there's a murder, right? They need to smoke."

"I suppose it would not be too much to ask, under the circumstances, that smokers segregate themselves to the staircase area?" Monica gave a galvanic, snorting chuckle, to show she was a good sport.

In the sudden silence, Mrs. Adler's voice could be heard. She had been telling Mrs. Spooner about how Milagros would probably never consent to return to the laundry room. Everyone heard her say, "I thought Teresa might be able to run a few loads for me?"

Ed Knowles now smoothly took control, raising his hands for

silence. "I think it might be appropriate if we began by having a moment of silence to commemorate Barn Seawright," he said.

"Why?" asked Maryanne. "Most of us never even knew him."

Her comments were politely ignored, and the moment of silence commenced. It was shattered, toward the end, by the whooping of an ambulance across the street and a noise suspiciously like that of stifled laughter from behind Allen's protective mask.

"Now then," said Ed Knowles. "We're here to discuss security, which is uppermost in all our minds just now. I'm sure Detectives Fields and Dumbrowski have impressed on all of you the need to be more vigilant than ever."

"Someone let a Chinese delivery boy in without asking," came an accusing voice from beneath the mailboxes. "It turned out he wanted the brownstone next door."

"Please!" cried Monica importantly. "Order! There will be plenty of time to state individual grievances over the course of—"

A babble of voices rose and swelled in the lobby, cutting her off, and Ed Knowles took a police whistle from his pocket and produced a shrill blast.

In the shocked silence, Mrs. Strabinski shouted, "The vissel! We all had one during the Tenants' Patrol, yes? I still have mine—"

"And, Ida," interposed Ed Knowles, "we're about to revitalize those whistles. The police think it's an excellent idea, in view of unsubstantiated rumors of a prowler."

"Unsub*stantiated?*" Maryanne's voice rose incredulously. "How much substantiation do you need? I would think old *Barn*'s remains in the GE would just about do it."

"I request permission to take the floor," said the voice they had all been dreading, and Mr. Crotty rose, before permission had been granted, and was seen to be withdrawing a sheaf of papers from a leather envelope. "I have important information," he said, "information which I have shared with the police. I want to go public now, as it were, and share it with you. Lest the ladies be alarmed, let me say that I am working with the police on this matter. Detectives Dumbrowski and Fields are fully cognizant of my findings, and are doing everything within their powers to ensure that we are protected."

For the next quarter hour, the tenants heard a somewhat scrambled version of Mr. Crotty's encounter with the apparition on the fire stairs. In his prepared statement, Mr. Crotty had glimpsed the shadowy figure at seven forty-five in the morning, as he was sacking his garbage. He had returned to his apartment and dialed the emergency number, 911, and been told that the presence of a half-seen prowler was not an emergency in New York City. Mr. Crotty had then gone both up and down the fire stairs, armed with a Samoan war club he happened to possess, and found it clean. The intruder had vanished.

"A Samoan war club?" asked Sarah Mason, half to herself.

"Which he just happens to *possess?*" answered Maryanne, more loudly.

"What I'd like to suggest," said Mr. Crotty, unperturbed, "is a concept I call Vertical Patrol. The way it would work is beautifully simple. I implemented it myself yesterday, but for Vertical Patrol to be really effective we would need additional volunteers. Men only, of course. We wouldn't want to subject the ladies to anything potentially dangerous."

There were a few timid hisses directed at Mr. Crotty's chauvinism, but most of the women present were only too happy to be excluded from his scheme. He was red-faced with importance now, gathering steam for his battle plan, like an old general recalled to the field after many years in retirement. He assumed an almost crouching position, ready for action, as he embarked on a detailed explanation.

"In Vertical Patrol, we would, of course, patrol the premises vertically. On the fire stairs and the regular stairs. At irregular times. You would never know when a member of the patrol was on duty—it might be at three in the afternoon, or it might be at midnight. The element of uncertainty is important. We would be equipped with a weapon of our choice, so long as it is legal. Baseball bats, flashlights, hammers . . . And of course we'd have our whistles. Any irregularity, and—" He pantomimed the act of raising a whistle to his lips with his left hand while brandishing a weapon with his right. Slowly, he let his hands drop to his sides and beamed at them. "Any recruits?" he asked.

"Tim, dear," said Allen, writhing in his leather chair, "isn't this a bit—excessive? I appreciate all your efforts on our behalf, but I have to say something. I just can't hold it back."

"By all means, Allen," said Mr. Crotty. "I welcome your input, as always."

"Well, frankly, if I was just skipping down the stairs to get the mail, say, without a thought in my mind? If I rounded the corner and saw you with your Samoan war club—if that actually happened—I might just, just *lose* it, if you see what I mean. It would be simply terrifying! Aren't we frightened enough without turning ourselves into bogeymen?"

Mr. Crotty opened his mouth to answer, but Ed Knowles seized the moment. "Most of the men in this building work a twelve- to fourteen-hour day, Mr. Crotty. We wouldn't have much time to participate in your vertical maneuvers. It seems dangerous to me to interfere with the police, who are trained for this sort of thing. While I admire your courage, I feel that—"

"*Shame!*" shouted Mrs. Strabinski, her strong voice carrying over all the others. "Mr. Crotty is the only hero here. If my Leon were alive, he'd be the first to join."

"Birds with a feather," murmured Monica. "Who's going to claim Mr. Seawright's body?"

"His sister, I understand," said Ed Knowles. "She's coming from Minneapolis."

Allen, wheezing, shuffled toward the elevator, and there was a general commotion of chair-folding and milling about which signified the breakup of the meeting. Ed Knowles distributed police whistles to the newer shareholders, looking embarrassed, and Monica hurried to Mr. Crotty, around whom a small coterie had formed. As usual in group meetings, nothing had been accomplished, and most of the participants seemed to want to disappear as quickly as possible.

The vivid quality of the murder, so thrilling in its way, had been leached of its immediate nature by Mr. Crotty's eccentric plan of action, and by the whistles. The whole thrust of Mr.

Crotty's program was too familiar to the old-timers, and too foreign to the new.

Sarah and Maryanne went upstairs with Allen, who urged them to come to his apartment for a while. Removing his surgical mask, he confided that he didn't really have the flu at all.

"In actual fact, I lost a cap on my front tooth just two hours before the meeting, and I'm *so* unsightly at the moment. Didn't want to frighten any of the old dears, and I couldn't bear to miss the fun, so—*voilà.*" He tossed the mask on a side table and left the room, reappearing with a bottle of wine and three glasses. "Until I get a temporary cap, I officially have the flu."

"Vanity," said Maryanne teasingly. "Isn't it one of the seven deadly sins?"

"Odd you should mention them, dear. I once played Wrath in a very fine production of *Dr. Faustus.* You know the scene, don't you, Sarah? Mephistopheles takes Faust down to hell and introduces him to the Seven Deadly Sins? He meets Wrath, Pride, Covetousness, Envy, Sloth, Gluttony, and Lechery. Each played by a different actor or actress, of course. I really wanted to play Sloth, but when I saw my costume I was so delighted I forgot my disappointment. It was all gorgeous, angry shades of scarlet and purple, and I made my entrance in a cloud of smoke—dry ice, for that effect—virtually screaming 'I am Wrath!' "

"What did Lechery wear?" asked Sarah.

"They had an actress, called her Lust instead of Lechery, and she was in a kind of acid green leotard, cut very low. Lust sounds so much nicer than Lechery, don't you think?"

"More wholesome, definitely," said Maryanne. "I think you have to be pretty old to get classed as a lecher."

"Everyone comfy?" Allen asked. Sarah was reclining on a slippery horsehair sofa, while Maryanne swung from the basket seat suspended from Douglas and Allen's ceiling. The apartment was furnished in an eclectic style, since both its owners had a fondness for Victoriana which collided oddly with their equal appreciation of found objects. The room was lit by several rose-shaded lamps which cast flattering pools of glowing light, illuminating here an onyx cigarette box, there a collection of worry beads from whose apex rose a large candle carved in the shape of Pope John XXIII, raising his hands in blessing. The candle had never been lit, because any melting would have resulted in the deformation of the Pope's miter.

"Well, if everyone's comfy, I'd like to say something," said Allen. "Personally, I'm scared. I didn't know Barnett Seawright very well, and what I knew I didn't like, but it scares me to hell and back that someone disliked him enough to murder him and put him in the same model refrigerator that Douglas and I have been cursing for over fifteen years."

"Fifteen years," said Maryanne. "Is that how long you've lived here?"

"Going on sixteen," said Allen. "We remember Monica when she was just approaching menopause."

"Eleven for me," said Maryanne, "and nine for Sarah. We've all lived here since it was practically a slum."

"When there was a laundromat on the corner," said Sarah dreamily, "and those coffee shops where you could get a cheese omelette for two-fifty. With toast and french fries."

"Exactly," said Allen. "I was even a waiter at the old Burger Hole, between acting jobs. You got not only the fries and toast, but also a slice of tomato and a cup of slaw with the omelette. It wasn't elegant, ladies, but it filled you up."

Maryanne was beginning to look angry, and Sarah wondered if she would reveal her counterterrorist activities to Allen. For Maryanne's sake, she hoped not; it seemed the fewer people who knew, the better. Allen was honorable and friendly, but he might find his neighbor's commando tactics too amusing to keep to himself.

"I remember those omelettes," she said quickly. "They were so delicious and greasy—they ruined me for the real thing. But you're digressing, Allen. You were saying that you felt afraid."

"Aren't you, dear?"

Sarah shrugged and tried to frame an honest reply. "Not really," she said. "I think it's because the whole thing seems so unreal. What do we have to do with rich characters like the bookstore landlord or Seawright?"

"Exactly," said Maryanne. "When this was a poorish neighborhood, back in Ida's Target Crime Area days, you worried about maybe getting mugged, or raped. Now it seems you have to be terribly affluent to end up in a store window or a castoff fridge. Is that a problem for anyone in this room?"

"You're assuming this killer is the way the *Post* makes him out to be," said Allen, forgetting about his missing front tooth and gesticulating with the hand he had been artfully draping before his mouth. "What if he doesn't distinguish between his victims? What if he blindly thinks everyone who lives in this neighborhood eats sushi and does arbitrage? The next victim could be one of you, or me, and it would all be for nothing. We'd have the worst of both worlds."

"Dead *and* poor," said Sarah. "I see what you mean."

For the next hour, they amused themselves by imagining fabulous injustices: Ida Strabinski shot down on Columbus Avenue because she was wearing the fur coat she had brought from Austria in 1936, or one of the building's au pair girls knifed on Broadway because she was carrying a shopping bag from an overpriced Food Emporium. Toward the end they became very silly, fabricating a tragedy in which Tim Crotty was strangled while on Vertical Patrol, on account of the priceless art treasure he carried, an object stolen from the Third World.

"His Samoan war club!" shrieked Maryanne. "An artifact sacred to the aboriginal people."

"But what about the intruder he claims to have seen on the fire stairs," said Allen when the laughter had died down. "Doesn't that give you a bit of a chill?"

"Poor old thing," said Sarah, slithering about on the horsehair. "I think he's taken to the drink. I think he imagines things, to make himself seem more important. There's no harm to it."

The phone rang then, and it was Douglas calling from Philadelphia, wanting to know how the meeting in the lobby had gone. Sarah and Maryanne took his call as the cue for their departure. They rode up in the elevator together, solemn and somehow depressed, despite their jolly time with Allen.

"Good night," said Maryanne, exiting first. "Lock up well."

And Sarah, sliding home the bolts and securing the chains of her own front door, wondered if she would obey the old impulse, the very one which shamed her, if she thought of it, and look under her bed before she climbed into it, to make sure no one was there.

SEVEN

The forbidden laundry room became quite an issue. For all their resources, most of the newer tenants were not allowed to have washers and dryers in their apartments—the water pressure was such that there had come a time when the system could handle no more. Ironically, Barnett Seawright had been the last shareholder to be allowed his own private laundry facilities.

Ruth Adler had tried to frame a polite request. Under the circumstances, that is to say, since Mr. Seawright's equipment would not now be used, couldn't she and her husband be granted the right—? No matter how she juggled the words, there was no way to make them tasteful. Besides, as common sense told her when reason returned, Seawright's estate would surely want the washer and dryer to remain. It increased the resale value.

Nobody seemed particularly eager to volunteer to serve on the Board. Before the Robin Hood Murders Joe had been planning to run for the next term. He had a number of constructive ideas—increasing the flip tax, raising the maintenance, and forbidding subletting among them—but even Joe seemed reluctant at the prospect of filling Barnett Seawright's chair. And there was the problem about Mr. Crotty, the only shareholder who had indicated that he might be willing to sit on the Board. How were they to gently dissuade him? Probably by maintaining the fiction that he was needed at the security end. And then what? Visions of Mr. Crotty ascending the stairs, war club poised, eyes glittering with the delusion that he was working with the police, gave Ruth the shudders. She had already lost her au pair, at least temporarily. Milagros had fled, on what Ruth thought of as compassionate leave, to an aunt up on St. Nicholas Avenue. She could not go back to her mother in Honduras, for fear of losing

her prospects of a green card. The law said that she must stay in
New York for eighteen months, and only nine of those months
had elapsed.

In the meantime, Ruth had worked out a reasonable agreement in which Jewel, Noreen, and Teresa took turns in airing
Megan and Phoebe in the park. On the whole, the children got
on, except for some quite extraordinary acting out on the part of
the Spooners' Jake, but the problem of the laundry remained.
Every day the wicker hamper in the girls' rooms grew fuller, for
Teresa had inexplicably refused to incorporate the Adler laundry with the Spooner items. Even for a consideration.

"Sure, it's after confusing me to sort out as it is," Teresa had
explained. "I'm awful sorry, Missus A, but it would altogether
destroy me."

Ruth had been reminded of a play, by Synge, she had been
forced to attend at Smith College. The black girls were no more
promising. She was sure they would call up other plays she had
seen in graduate school. Passing through the hall one night, she
had heard one of her daughters sleepily singing behind the
closed bedroom door. The voice had been guttural, unnatural, as
if Megan or Phoebe had been possessed.

My grandfather mar-eeed one fine St. Kitts wo-mann, growled the
voice of one of Ruth Adler's daughters, seeming world weary
and totally foreign. It repeated the lyric over and over, as if it
knew no others, but was desperately trying to perfect itself.

When Ruth opened the door and peered inside, she saw her
girls asleep against their pillows, bathed in the glow of the
Gladys Goose lamp. All was well.

Only the problem of the laundry was real, and eventually
Ruth, who was a practical woman, gathered her daughters'
soiled garments in a bag, loaded it into a shopping cart, and took
it herself to the sole surviving laundromat on Columbus. When
she had loaded the machine and taken her place on the long
wooden bench, a curious feeling began to envelop her. She knew
she ought to make use of the half hour—certainly she could not
just sit and watch the garments as they were thrown up and
sucked back in the froth of detergent. She could be reading the
new issue of *Publisher's Weekly,* if only she had thought to bring

it. Now that she was so rarely on the premises at New Age Books, she was compelled to prove that she was twice as knowledgeable as the Monday-to-Friday crowd, who were not at her level. She might also profit by a stroll to the Food Emporium, which had a reasonably good selection of cheeses.

The fact that she did neither—return to the apartment and arm herself with productive reading materials, or walk two blocks to replenish her larder in anticipation of the weekend dinner party—convinced her that she had entered into a peculiar plane of feeling.

The stale warmth and steamy atmosphere of the laundromat did not repel or enervate her, as she had expected it to do. It seemed strangely familiar, and attractive in a shaming sort of way. It reminded her of her undergraduate days, when she had loved the concept of Great Literature and also belonged to the Modern Dance Club. It reminded her of the laundry room in the dorms, where she had eaten Snickers bars and read the Lucia novels. It belonged to the time in her life which she could fairly label *Before I pulled myself together and went for my MBA.*

Ruth resisted the arcane seductiveness of her uninformed and wholly unpractical young womanhood, and left the laundromat in search of some meaningful way to pass the needed time, but again a strange impulse overtook her. She crossed the street and entered the chaotic and underachieving premises of Food World, where she stood in a very long line to purchase one item.

People magazine was what she had chosen, and she sat in a sort of idiotic and contented trance, reading it, until Megan and Phoebe's clothes were returned to her, clean, dry, and fragrant.

Some of the women in the building, spearheaded by Mrs. Spooner, decided not to wear their fur coats out anymore, even though another cold snap had set in. Nobody wanted to present a seemly target for the Robin Hood Killer. "Why advertise it?" Fay Spooner asked. "Why let them know your income bracket?" And indeed, in an old down coat and the stained sneakers she had been about to throw away, she looked almost disreputable.

Sarah had no fur coat to hide, only her guilty secret about the telephone call from Gordon Childs. It seemed to her impossible that *she* might be singled out for attack, and she felt no particular fear on that account, but her spirits seemed to plunge lower and lower with every passing, lusterless day. Her London piece was completed, and she had another assignment, for a women's magazine, which she could hardly bear to contemplate. It was to be called "Grapes of Rath" and would be a profile of Holly Rath, a California vineyard heiress who was currently living in New York, hoping to become this year's hottest performance artist.

It seemed that her life had rolled down a gentle hill, so slowly she had not sensed the descent, and had now come to a rest in an airless pocket, or depression. It had been arrested in this position for some time now, but she hadn't noticed until the grotesque murders had forced her to look around and up from her entrenched outpost, right on the fringes of what had become life in Manhattan.

How could she imagine she had been, if not happy, content? She had not missed her married life, which had so degenerated toward the end she had welcomed the divorce as an opportunity to see the man she had once loved as a normal, flawed human being instead of the monster of deceit and arrogance he had begun to seem. In a limited way, she could even be friends with Mark now, if his university had not sent him off on sabbatical to the Shetland Islands.

The unavailability of suitable men she had long accepted as a given, and the few little blighted romances she had conducted since the end of her marriage seemed plucky rather than truly sad. If she tried to analyze it, she came up with one really disturbing fact: nothing stirred her to passion. The articles she wrote were at best mildly amusing or of minimal useful social impact. At worst they were—like the proposed Holly Rath piece —loathsome puffs designed to appeal to people she would not even want to know.

All around her she seemed to see people who embodied the concept of commitment. The dress-for-success wives seemed bound to reproduce and also get partnerships or die in the attempt, while their au pairs braved hostile climates and unlovely work conditions in the hopes of emerging with a green card. Even Maryanne, who lacked the drive to become a phenomenal photographer's rep, had found her niche as a counterterrorist. It didn't matter that Maryanne's acts of guerrilla warfare were quite possibly insane, any more than Mr. Crotty's loony zeal could be tarnished by its looniness. They were passionate! Committed! Partnerships, green cards, Vertical Patrol . . . what did it matter? They were all the same, when all was said and done. They represented the culmination of a yearning, and Sarah was in mourning because she yearned for nothing she could name. She was thinking she would willingly trade her nominal sanity for Maryanne's desire to injure offending cars or furs, when she heard an important voice blaring from her living room.

It was the voice of the anchorman on the evening news, and he was telling her that the coroner had at last issued a statement concerning the landlord in the bookstore window.

"About time," said Sarah, turning the flame under her boil-in-the-bag cheese-and-broccoli to low and sprinting into the next room.

The mournful-looking coroner was engaged in a duet with a reporter who wore her hair in a jaunty cockscomb and hissed her esses. "Then it appears that Mr. Muellen's death was due to entirely natural causes?" urged the reporter.

A great deal of medical jargon ensued, in which the coroner appeared to say that the landlord in the window had suffered a fatal coronary occlusion, sometime between midnight and 1:30 A.M. on the night in question. The contents of his stomach had revealed massive and only partially digested amounts of food substances, suggesting that he had eaten a hearty Japanese meal not long before his death. Contusions to the head, although not in themselves severe enough to have caused death, had obfuscated the proceedings. Every avenue had to be explored.

As the screen changed to scenes of a bombing in Beirut, the phone began to ring.

"You see," said the voice of Gordon Childs resignedly when Sarah lifted the receiver. "You see what I'm up against? I weigh one hundred and thirty pounds, and that mother was a whale!"

Sarah formulated several questions and was silent, waiting.

"I didn't mean to crack his head," said Gordon. "It was just so *awkward* getting him into that window. You have no idea, Sarah, it was simply exhausting, with his head weaving every which way and his body not cooperating and his legs dead weight—"

"Gordon!" cried Sarah.

"You heard the coroner," said Gordon righteously. "Mr. Muellen had a natural death. I never meant to mark him up."

Fay Spooner crouched at her window, observing something strange through her opera glasses. She had been looking out, hoping for a glimpse of the mailman, who was unaccountably late, when Teresa had come into view. The girl was ambling up from the Broadway end of the street, swinging the bag which contained Fay's dry cleaning. There was nothing exceptional in this, and certainly Fay would never have gone for the opera glasses simply to monitor Teresa's progress. It was what happened when the au pair reached the building's canopy—the darting out of a very tall, very black man who seemed to be detaining her in conversation.

It was infuriating, because the man and his captive audience moved in and out of her line of vision, sometimes retreating beneath the canopy and becoming quite invisible. At first Fay had supposed the man might be the black detective assigned to the murder case, but he was both older and much better dressed. Teresa shifted the dry cleaning from arm to arm, nodding, smiling, and seeming to answer questions, for the man was writing something in a small notebook. Fay was sure he was not one of the local television reporters, but he could be a newspaperman. What else could account for his jottings?

She hoped Teresa was not providing him with juicy background material for some scurrilous piece on the Robin Hood Killer, artlessly babbling on about the human frailties of the building's shareholders. That would be even worse than her other suspicion—that Teresa was being courted by some relation or acquaintance of one of the colored au pairs. Or would it? Fay was ashamed to admit that her mind had spun a little scenario in which Teresa, on her day off, had introduced the Spooner family to a strapping Island male named Chauncey or Trevor, an intimidating specimen of manhood who would chuckle warmly while casing the apartment for vulnerable silver or easily fenced electronic equipment.

Where were they? They had vanished beneath the canopy again, still locked in their interminable conversation. Or had Teresa, against all instruction, admitted him to the building? There were very strict rules about allowing strangers into the building, rules which had been drafted before Fay and her family had bought their apartment. The rules were one of the reasons she had been persuaded by her husband to ignore the terrible lack of a doorman. She had been raised on Park Avenue, where the kindly and avuncular doorman had been a totem of her youth. Jim, the doorman from County Mayo who had guarded her parents' building, was the very reason she had opted for an au pair from Ireland. It had seemed the traditional, the *homey* choice. Why, then, did Teresa make her uneasy? The reason was one she did not, could not acknowledge, and so she told herself that the girl was too open and friendly for her own good and for the good of Fay's children. She could imagine her striking up conversations with inappropriate and possibly dangerous individuals in Central Park, while Jake and Freddie were entrusted to her care. The very possibility, coupled with her nervousness over the conversation taking place beneath the canopy, made Fay long for a drink. But it was not yet two in the afternoon, and one couldn't, really, not even the smallest spill of vodka in harmless orange juice. Fay had discovered how nicely life passed by when it was brightened with frequent infusions of vodka, but the trouble was that she never wanted to stop once she'd begun. Even a very judicious pacing would not ensure sobriety by dinnertime—not if she started now.

Good. The man was walking away and Teresa would be on her way up. Fay returned the opera glasses and went to the kitchen phone, which she lifted and placed to her ear. This way she could hang up when Teresa entered the apartment, calling a cheery good-bye as if she had been engaged in a productive and pleasant conversation.

When she heard the key turn in the lock, she released a musical little laugh and said, "Fine, then. I'm looking forward to it. Next Tuesday. See you then." She laughed again and trilled a good-bye as Teresa entered the kitchen and placed the dry cleaning on the table.

"Here ye go, Missus Ess," said Teresa. "I'll just be off to collect the boys now." Her cheeks were pink from the wind off Riverside Drive, and despite the punk hair and the distressed denim jacket she wore, she looked as wholesome as a dairymaid.

"Teresa, dear," said Fay, striving for a casual tone, "who was that man you were talking to in front? I was looking out for the mailman, and I couldn't help noticing him."

"You *would* notice him," said Teresa with enthusiasm. "He was altogether great! His name is Terry, same as one of my brothers, and he's a sociologist, doing a survey, he said."

"What sort of a survey?" Fay felt she had gauged the situation correctly after all. The man was a journalist, intent on gathering information for a story on the Robin Hood killings.

"An ethnic check," said Teresa. "He wanted to know if this building was integrated, you know?"

Fay remembered belatedly that Teresa had a degree in history from some college in Ireland. It was one of the reasons she had been so eager to sponsor her. She was honestly sorry that her au pair girl's devotion to study had availed her nothing in the land of her birth, but also glad that Freddie and Jake would benefit as a result.

"I hope you told him that the building is fully integrated," she said, smiling. She hoped the girl could not divine that her mind was racing with unasked questions. Was the man simply a black version of a yellow journalist who would try to cast aspersions on their co-op after convincing the gullible Teresa that he was a bona fide sociologist? Or was he a confederate of the actual killer, preparing information for the deadly Robin Hood? Teresa was taking an age to answer, so she smiled harder.

"Well, I just filled him in on a few things—put him in the picture," said Teresa. "For example, he said he could tell about some of the names on the intercom, but others were trickier."

Fay felt that she would have benefited by being allowed to scream very loudly, but she could not permit herself such a luxury, any more than she could succumb to the need for a nice drink so early in the afternoon. "Tell *which* things?" she asked. "Could you be a bit more specific, Teresa?"

"He said it was clear about the name Francini, that it was Italian, and others was surely Jewish, and of course the super's is Hispanic, but what was he to make of certain names? They could be WASPy names, but then again they might belong to blacks."

"What names might those be, do you remember?" Fay had known a very refined colored girl in college, a doctor's daughter from Indiana called Marla Mason. "I suppose he could have been referring to Sarah Mason," she said.

Teresa reached behind her and reflectively stroked the polyethylene bag containing Fay's dry cleaning. "Mason was one of the names," she admitted. "Also Platt and Knowles and yer own name, Mrs. Spooner. Who's to tell, see what I mean?"

Fay felt obscurely frightened, as if Teresa and the unknown man had accused Spooner ancestors of engaging in the slave trade and passing on their surname to freemen now living in Manhattan. This was so obviously ridiculous that she beat out a sharp tattoo with her fingernails against the tiled counter.

"I think it might have been the tiniest bit *irresponsible* for you to have carried on this conversation with a perfect stranger, someone who might not have our best interests at heart," she said in tones of informed authority. "We are, after all, living in a building where a murder has been committed, and where a police investigation is being carried out. Isn't that so, Teresa?"

"Ah, not to worry, Missus Ess! Sure, Terry has nothing to do with the trouble, nothing a'tall." She smiled kindly and then consulted her watch and said it was surely time to fetch Jake and Freddie from play group, wasn't it?

Fay followed her to the door. "Did you mention Mrs. McCoy?" she asked as Teresa was in the act of pulling the door open. Edwina McCoy was a black fashion model who spent most of her time these days in Europe. She had bought the penthouse across from Barnett Seawright's when the building had been converted.

"Who's that then? Who's Mrs. McCoy?"

Teresa seemed genuinely interested, but the elevator had arrived, and in the face of Mrs. Spooner's attitude of defeat, her decision not to answer the question about the McCoy woman, she shrugged and entered the elevator. Jake and Freddie would be waiting, and wasn't that the important thing on her agenda? Next thing she knew, Missus Ess would be asking about Jewel and Norrie and Milagros, and wondering if *their* presence on the premises didn't constitute the concept of perfect, and full, integration?

EIGHT

It was midafternoon of the following day when a terrible and frightening sound was heard issuing from one of the upper floors of the building. It sounded as if a whole crew of people were up there, because, punctuated with frantic blasts of a police whistle, two or three voices were shouting for help.

Standing at her door, preparing to lock it as she left, Sarah Mason could make out the voice of Monica calling "Thief! Thief!" Then the whistle was blown, a long, protracted shrill, and a deeper voice took up the cry of "Thief!" The poky elevator was nowhere in sight, so Sarah reluctantly began to sprint up the back stairs. She could hear other feet on the stairs now, and the sound of Ernesto's service elevator cranking into action. Now the deeper voice was shouting "I've been robbed! I've been robbed!"

When she finally attained the landing of Monica's floor and raced round the corner, she saw only one person, the one she'd expected to see, but where were the others? Monica stood, tears streaming down her cheeks, blasting on her whistle. The door to her apartment stood open, and Sarah could see no evidence of a violent robbery. As she approached Monica, wondering if she would have to remove the whistle from her mouth by force, she was joined by Ernesto, who raced from the cab of the service elevator and came to a scudding halt by her side. The other elevator came groaning up and disgorged Allen, his mouth agape with alarm. Sarah was glad to see that his tooth had been recapped. All three of them approached Monica, and it was Allen who gently removed the whistle, wiped it rather fastidiously on the sleeve of Monica's coat, and dropped it into her handbag, which she was clutching protectively.

"Now, dear," he said in soothing tones. "What's happened?"

"It's a terrible violation," gasped Monica. "I feel as if I had been raped."

Ernesto, hearing only the dread verb, looked both horrified and mildly disbelieving. "Someone attack you, Mrs. Platt? Someone hurt you?"

Monica shook her head violently and indicated that they should follow her into her apartment. After the locks and bolts had been shot, the little party went into Monica's dining room and took seats at her large, ornate dining table. "I had just returned from a *sojourn,*" she said. "I took off, removed, my coat and hat and gloves, and then I went into the kitchen to put the kettle on for a cup of instant coffee. I like to have coffee when I return after a sojourn, especially in the afternoons."

Sarah became aware of the sound of the kettle, screaming away unobserved in the far reaches of Monica's kitchen, and went to turn the flame down. She knew it would be the neighborly thing to do to make Monica and the others a refreshing cup, but she didn't want to miss out on Monica's explanation of this extraordinary carry-on.

When she returned, Allen filled her in. "Monica says she thought it would be a good idea to go back to her bedroom and slip into some comfier shoes, and that's when she saw she'd been robbed."

"Come and see for yourselves," said Monica. "Witness this terrible act of vandals for yourselves."

Monica's bedroom had indeed been invaded. Someone had riffled through her clothing and tossed it to the floor, and the drawers of her bureau were cracked open carelessly, as if the thief had pawed through the contents and, not finding anything of value, simply shoved them in anger. One of the little end tables at the side of her bed lay on its side, and an alarm clock lay many feet away, proof of the violence with which the intruder had conducted his search. The window had been smashed, and Monica repeated many times that the thief had "utilized" the fire escape to do his cowardly and dastardly work. Since the fire escape serviced only the rear apartments, and since there was no access to it from the sealed-off courtyard, Sarah felt uneasy.

"Maybe we better call the police," suggested Ernesto.

"But let's establish what's been taken first," said Allen.

"Oh, the violation," said Monica. "He's laid his fingers on my most intimate things. Garments I wear next to my flesh!" Distractedly, she knelt on the carpeted floor and picked up a pair of burnt orange trousers, caressing them as if they had been the victim of unspeakable tragedy. Ernesto looked discreetly away.

Sarah and Allen made a survey of the other rooms and could find no damage, but since they had no way of knowing what shelf or cranny might have contained a treasure, now missing, they came back to the bedroom. Monica was hunched over a large, sandalwood jewelry box, replacing scattered objects and making an inventory. Ceramic earrings and costume necklaces, retrieved by Ernesto from the far corners of the room, were being laid to rest.

"Wait," said Sarah. "Shouldn't you leave everything just as you found it? For the police?"

"They'll want to take photographs, won't they?" Monica brightened and threw the turquoise bracelet she had been returning at her feet. "I acquired *that* little item in Santa Fe," she informed them, smiling in a most un-Monica-like way. "Otto— Mr. Platt—bargained those Indians down from the original price."

Rage, Sarah saw, had deprived Monica of her usual extravagance of speech. She had always considered Monica a fool, and fool she might still be, but Monica's grief at the rude invasion of her privacy was very real.

Together they trooped from room to room, and it soon became apparent that the thief had been inexperienced. A silver-plated cake stand was missing, as was a small pitcher of cranberry glass. Monica groaned at these discoveries, but without the genuine sadness Sarah had detected in the figure bent over the sandalwood box.

"What a shame poor Tim can't be here," Allen murmured to Sarah. "He would have so enjoyed taking charge."

Mr. Crotty, as they both knew, had taken to whiling the afternoons away in the only working-class bar that remained on Columbus Avenue.

"It's true," Sarah said, trying not to wince at the painting she had just noticed in the living room. It was a portrait of a younger Monica, grandly dressed in an electric blue gown showing much décolletage. She could hear Ernesto on the telephone, summoning the police, and she suddenly remembered the cacophony of voices she had heard between the blasts of the police whistle.

"Monica," she called, "wasn't there someone else up here when we arrived?"

Monica entered the living room, carrying a gravy ladle. It was very ornate, and she held it as a queen might her scepter. "This was presented to me on the occasion of my wedding," she explained, "by a very dear friend, now deceased. I'm just grateful it was overlooked." When Sarah repeated the question Monica looked puzzled at first, and then blushed becomingly and giggled. "It was the deep-breathing exercise," she explained. "Between blowing the whistle and calling for help, I performed an exercise which helps to bring out the deeper chest tones. It's basically an aid to combat symptoms of the anxious."

"Well, dear," said Allen, "I think you're back to normal now. I really must fly, have an appointment, so if nobody minds—?"

"Oh, but you're a material witness, Allen." Monica looked as if she might cry.

"So am I," said Sarah, sighing. "I'll stay."

Since it was Milagros' first day back, she correctly judged that not much would be expected of her. The awful nightmares she had been prepared to endure had not come, after all, and the days up on St. Nicholas Avenue with her Auntie Marta had only strengthened her conviction—she was destined for a life in the center of Manhattan, an upwardly mobile life which had to have, as its springboard, her job in this building. The nanny room didn't seem so small, after all, and her private bathroom seemed almost festive. Auntie Marta's bathroom was thick with droppings from the ring-necked doves she kept and sometimes allowed to fly freely through the rooms. And another thing was that it was quite frequently so cold that Milagros could see her breath in the apartment on St. Nicholas Avenue. All in all, she preferred life at the Adlers'. Even if she would never be able to forget the lifeless eyes of the nasty gringo in the refrigerator, she was at least warm and well-fed here, and that was surely something.

Except for Phoebe, she had the place to herself. The senior Adlers were both out, he at his job and she at the health club. Megan was at her play group and would be for another hour. Milagros had settled Phoebe at the kitchen table with some water paints and plenty of newspaper to soak up the spillage Phoebe would certainly, perhaps spitefully, produce.

She had not seen any of the shareholders in the lobby or on the elevator, but Ernesto had told her about the robbery in the Monica woman's apartment. She had felt panic beginning to overtake her at this evidence of a new crime, but then reason prevailed. The Adler apartment was in the front of the building and had no fire escape, so she was relatively safe. Still, she felt sure that an evil and malevolent force was at work in the building. It had killed the equally evil and malevolent Seawright man and wanted something from the Monica woman, who impressed Milagros as merely foolish, but who could tell?

Phoebe seemed engrossed in her painting, and Milagros made a decision. Silently, she opened the refrigerator door and took one of the extra-large eggs from its oval depression. She swung the door back and made her way to the nanny room. From her oversized handbag she withdrew an object wrapped in newspaper and a thick candle. Working swiftly, she assembled the little shrine on her bedside table. She sprinkled it with some of the powder her aunt had thoughtfully tipped into a box which had once contained earplugs, and then went to her bathroom and filled the little box with water. Her aunt practiced a half-assed form of *santaría* and was not nearly up to the *bruja* status of her mother, but Marta was here and Mama's next letter might not arrive for a week, depending on what she was up to back home. Better some form of protection than none at all.

She had performed the water ritual and lit the candle, and was kneeling in front of the shrine, the egg clasped in both her hands, when the words of the incantation were driven away by the voice of Phoebe, quite close.

"Do you have any M&Ms?"

Milagros blew the candle out and turned around, squatting on her heels, hoping that her body blocked the statuette from Phoebe's prying eyes.

"You know your mother doesn't like for you to have candy," she said. "If you're hungry you can have carrots and celery, Phoebe. You know where they are."

Phoebe moved a few steps into the nanny room. She looked very confident.

"You're not supposed to come into my room," said Milagros. "This is my private room."

"Why are you holding an egg, Milagros? Is that one of Mommy's eggs? Did you take it from the refrigerator while I was painting?"

"I was going to put it back," said Milagros, and then, infuriated at being cross-examined by a small girl in a *New Yorker* T-shirt, "Get *out* of here, Phoebe. I'll be back in the kitchen in a minute."

"It's so smokey in here," said Phoebe. "I saw you blow that candle out. What are you doing, Milagros?"

"None of your business, Phoebe."

"Mommy doesn't allow smoking in our apartment," said Phoebe virtuously. "I bet she wouldn't want you to be playing with candles, either."

"Okay," said Milagros, thinking frantically. "When we go pick Megan up, we'll stop and get some M&Ms at the candy store." She was sure the greedy child would acquiesce to the bribe, but Phoebe's fascination at the strange rites in the nanny room overcame her sweet tooth.

"Is that Jesus?" she asked, peering around Milagros and pointing to the little figure at the center of the shrine. "We don't believe in him, you know. Is that Jesus?"

"Not exactly," said Milagros.

"Well, but who is he?" Phoebe had sunk to her haunches and looked prepared to stay for the duration. "Who *is* he?" she repeated, clutching at the bedspread and leaving traces of cadmium blue.

"I'm just playing a game," said Milagros. "Something you wouldn't understand."

Phoebe squinted, marshaling the available evidence. For a time, Milagros thought it would be too much for her to put the components of the alien scene into some sort of order, but her hopes were dashed when Phoebe said:

"You don't play games with eggs. Everybody knows that. I don't know a single game you play with *eggs.*"

In the end, it was easier to woo Phoebe with *santaría* than with chocolate. Milagros tried to make it as bland as possible, speaking of evil spirits and the need for protection, but Phoebe was not an easy adversary. When Milagros spoke of the egg as a symbol of perfect wholeness and regeneration, Phoebe countered with something called Eggs Benedict, asking how brunch could make a person safe?

Milagros felt herself bested. She had never paid much attention to the spiritual things which were her mother's legacy, and thought of her aunt as a rank novice. For the first time she wished, fervently, to have understood the need to pass a snake on the occasion of her first menstruation. That, at least, would have shut Phoebe up. She rambled on, producing for her young inquisitor the more lurid aspects of her mother's religion.

"*Chickens?*" Phoebe gasped. "Oven-stuffer roasters?"

"Live chickens," said Milagros, rising to her feet and clucking crazily, imitating the self-important gait of domestic fowl.

Phoebe regarded her, wide-eyed, and backed out of the nanny room. Milagros dismantled the shrine and prepared to right the potential havoc she had unleashed. A stop at the candy store was definitely called for. She wished she could ask her mother if chocolate destroyed brain cells and clouded the memory of children.

Riding down on the elevator, Phoebe shuddered and whispered, "*Chickens.*"

"Look, Phoebe," said Milagros when they were in shouting distance of the candy store, "it's just a way of getting what you want."

"Anything?" asked Phoebe, tightening her mittened grasp in a sudden, spasmodic gesture.

"Anything," said Milagros.

Sarah saw Milagros and the older Adler child going up Columbus as she was making her way into Food World. She hadn't realized Milagros was back on the job, and wondered if the burglary would further disturb her. Inside the supermarket was clogged with customers, bulky in coats which were all several sizes too large, as fashion now dictated. Each cash register had a long, grumbling line backed up and reaching into the aisles, which made maneuvering a shopping cart even more difficult than normal.

The temperature had dropped again and a light snow was predicted. "When can my window be replaced?" Monica had wanted to know. "I'd freeze to hypothermia in my bedroom." Sarah had suggested that the vandalized bedroom be sealed off, temporarily, and that Monica sleep in the spare room. She knew it would have been more charitable to offer her own spare room, but she had a book review to complete. It was on account of this review that she had come to stock up on tinned and frozen food; experience had taught her that the best way to write a review was to hole up for three days, the first two for reading the book and making notes, the last for the actual writing. She had been about to stock her cupboards when Monica's cries for help waylaid her, and now it was three hours later and she was feeling panicky and irritable. So much so, in fact, that she almost failed to notice Maryanne, who was bending over the new cheese section Food World had recently installed.

Maryanne was examining the cheeses, her face set in lines of disapproval. Once she lifted a double-cream, examined the price tag, and literally threw it back onto the shelves, uttering a cry of what sounded like outrage.

"Engaging in acts of counterterrorism?" said Sarah by way of greeting. "Bruising the overpriced *fromage?*"

Maryanne turned around with a bitterly bright smile. "Hi," she said. "What's new?"

"Monica's apartment was broken into this afternoon," said

Sarah, and then, because they were blocking the flow of traffic, they wheeled their carts to the end of the Dairy aisle and Sarah sketched in the details of the robbery.

"Did Dumbrowski and Fields come?"

"No, they weren't available. It was filed as a break-and-enter, I guess. The cops didn't seem too interested when it turned out the perp had only taken a cake stand and a pitcher."

"What kind of pitcher?"

"Cranberry glass."

"I *like* cranberry glass," said Maryanne. "Do I have to stop liking it because Monica had one?"

"You can't be a counterterrorist and a snob both," said Sarah. "The thing that bothers me is, how did he get in by the fire escape?"

"Meaning you think it had to be an inside job?" Maryanne jounced her cart smartly and smiled. "Can you think of anyone in our building who would go to all that trouble to pinch a plate cake stand and a pretty pitcher?"

Sarah thought for a moment of the au pairs, the only people in the building who might be innocent enough to think these humble objects valuable or desirable simply as pretty acquisitions, but she could not really imagine the four girls as cat burglars. She shook her head. "Maybe the burglar expected to find money, or jewels? Maybe he ransacked the room and was so disgusted at the slim pickings he just meandered through the rest of the apartment and grabbed two things that pleased him, as compensation."

"I don't think so," said Maryanne. "Why concentrate on Monica's bedroom? Why didn't he toss the whole place? I'll tell you why. Whoever broke into Missus Malaprop's place *expected* to find something in the bedroom. When it wasn't there, he considered his options. He or she, I should say, but let's call it 'he.' He could replace all the things he'd flung about, make it look as if nobody had ever been there—"

"Not with the broken window," said Sarah.

"Don't be so literal," cried Maryanne, looking genuinely cross, as if Sarah had become the overpriced cheese. "Broken windows, by themselves, can be blamed on all sorts of things, but garments don't fly out of closets on their own, do they? No. The perp took two of Monica's little treasures to make it *look* like a burglary."

Sarah had toyed with this idea herself, but she was suddenly tired by the subject of Monica's paltry losses. The Robin Hood Murderer seemed far less important than her deadline for the book review, and she still had to pay a visit to the last remaining cobbler on Columbus Avenue to redeem her reheeled snow boots.

"I'll tell you this," hissed Maryanne. "I wouldn't want to be Ed Knowles. He's the last one left."

NINE

The original charter for the Board of Directors had provided for five, and five they had been until quite recently. Barnett Seawright had been the current President of the sitting Board, with Monica as Recording Secretary. Douglas had been Vice President, but he had resigned in high dudgeon over an ironclad sublet clause the others had voted in. A very grand old lady, Tess Abelson, had been head of operations, but her death in an aisle of Food World had saddened everyone at Thanksgiving time.

Ed Knowles was the fifth member and, together with Barnett, he embodied the spirit of the new order. Ed was efficient and affable. He teased old Mrs. Abelson and tolerated Monica, and sparred, in extremely enlightened ways, with Douglas. If some in the building thought him smarmy, there were always others eager to point out that Ed Knowles was the perfect choice for bridging the gap between the old tenants and the new. If Ed Knowles, like Barnett Seawright, secretly craved a doorman, at least he was apologetic about it. Where Seawright could be abrasive, Ed was always conciliatory. It was Ed Knowles who had proven his point, when announcing his candidacy for the Board, by saying that he liked the building *exactly as it is.*

Maryanne pondered the power plays of the Board as she prepared for bed that evening. When Douglas resigned, numerous shareholders had pointed out that the Board was hardly equipped to vote on any issues, since they were four. In the event of a tie, there would be no fifth party to cast the deciding vote. Maryanne, rubbing Night-time Oil of Olay on her face with the approved upward strokes, tried to remember what excuse had been offered. Someone, it seemed, had promised to run at the next elections, in January. That was now only a week away, on the last Tuesday in the month. Who was it who had promised to run?

Maryanne closed her eyes, brushing her hair with a natural-bristle brush. Even though she was now thirty-eight years old, she constantly experienced guilt at stopping short of the hundred strokes her mother had always demanded before bedtime. Well, hey, her mother had lived in rural New York State, where the air was clear and unpolluted. If Mrs. Francini were alive today she would have to know that one hundred strokes in Manhattan would produce hair so oily nothing short of twice-daily washings could delube it. Hair. That Honduran au pair certainly had beautiful hair. Milagros. Miracle. Worked for—the Adlers! That was it. Joe Adler, an uptight, glad-handing Yuppie if ever she'd seen one, *he* was the man who had promised to run. Oh, very much to Seawright's taste Joe Adler would be. Damn the lower-income tenants and full speed ahead—twenty-four-hour swing-shift doormen, maintenance increases, wild orchids in the lobby, and marble floors in the laundry room. Protecting his investment, he'd call it.

Maryanne threw the brush down and marched to her refrigerator. Anger never failed to make her hungry, and she assembled a little plate of downscale cheese, crackers, and radishes. Sitting at her kitchen table, she concentrated all her energies on the nagging question of the Board's composition. Fair enough, they were prepared to wait until the January elections—anything to avoid Mr. Crotty as a temporary stopgap. But then old Mrs. Abelson had died, and they were reduced to three. Surely something in the corporation's bylaws forbade so small a body of rulers?

It was only midnight, and she thought Sarah would still be up, but calling Sarah seemed the wrong thing to do. For one thing, Sarah seemed preoccupied; for another, her normally orderly writer's mind did not seem to respond to the current crime wave as nimbly as it might have done. Maryanne reached for the notepad she kept next to the kitchen telephone and began to jot down notes between bites of radish and cheese. She wrote down the names of the Board members as they had been before natural death, murder, and defection had reduced them.

After Mrs. Abelson's name she inked in a star, to show that Tess's inclinations had compared favorably with her own. Dippy Monica got a star, and so did Douglas. After the names of Barnett Seawright and Ed Knowles she drew a swastika. She thought she saw a pattern, but when you crossed off the Board members who had left—by whatever means—you ended up with one star and one swastika. A sort of grotesque balance of power was being maintained.

She tore off another piece of paper and rearranged her quotient. One of the people in her camp had left voluntarily, while the other had succumbed to cardiac infarction in Food World. The member of the enemy camp was the only one who had been forcibly removed by an unknown agent, and this didn't suit her embryo theory at all. She had half thought to find a pattern in which sympathetic shareholders had been intimidated from serving on the Board, freeing the way for the New Order to turn her building into a bastion for Yuppies, but if the Greed King of them all, Seawright, had been stabbed to death and packed into an ancient fridge, what possible sense could her theory make?

She knew that Monica had been kept on because she could be bullied, and Monica provided the odd vote, in the old equation. With Ed and "Barn" at her throat, mightn't Monica crumble and toss her precious vote in with theirs?

Maryanne switched on the overhead light and went to the dining room, where portfolios of her clients' work and correspondence of all kinds reposed on what had been her dining room table in the days of her marriage. Grateful for the knee socks she wore under her nightshirt, now that the heat was winding down, she methodically searched for Monica's last Newsletter. Proper minutes from the meetings of the Board of Directors arrived from the Managing Agent, but Monica's Newsletter, so amusing in its ungrammatical asides and grandiose prose, was always slipped beneath the door. It was easy to find the November newsletter, which had a turkey decal affixed to the top, and the one for December, which featured both candy canes tied with a green bow, and the words:

In this joyous season, let us not forget Mrs. Theodora Abelson, who passed away. Her gallant and vivacious Spirit graced our building for 1/4 of a Century, and those of us familiar with Tess's caring and cheerful smile will miss her.

The rest of the December newsletter indicated that elevator repairs were to be discussed at the next meeting. The crumbling of certain portions of the building's facade were also to be tackled in January, when contractor's bids had been compared, and there was mention of something Monica referred to as "lavatory flushometers," apparently having to do with water pressure complaints. The usual dreary stuff, thought Maryanne. Nothing revealing here, but why was there no newsletter from the January meeting? Monica was generally very prompt.

Maryanne drifted to the kitchen and poured herself a glass of wine. Was there anything unusual in not receiving the newsletter? The minutes from the Managing Agent, dry and terse, had arrived slightly late, and addressed the operational problems outlined in the December newsletter. These minutes, unlike Monica's missives, were never even slightly personal, sentimental, in nature, and for a moment Maryanne wondered if her neighbor had not performed her secretarial duties because of an ethical problem. Mightn't Monica have drawn the line at mourning, in print, the demise of Barnett Seawright? Since his smile had been neither caring nor cheerful, and there had been nothing pleasant to remember him by, perhaps Monica had found herself in the grip of writer's block?

Trying to ignore the whooping of an ambulette, Maryanne went, glass in hand, to test the water pressure in her three toilets. All performed serviceably, but that was because she lived on the fifth floor. It was the tenants on the higher floors who were experiencing difficulties. She supposed it was something to be grateful for, not having to deal with flushometers, but somehow it didn't seem enough.

Ruth Adler felt everything was coming apart. That was the only expression she could think of that came near to describing her almost continual state of anxiety. She knew it was unfair, but she thought she could pinpoint the moment when it had started. That moment was not, as people might assume if invited to guess, the occasion of the murder of Barnett Seawright. It had been dreadful, of course, and somehow the fact that *her* au pair had been the one to discover him made it subtly worse, but the unraveling feeling had been with her for some time before.

Admit it, she told herself. Things had begun to come apart soon after Milagros had come to live with them. The girl had brought trouble with her in some sense Ruth could scarcely comprehend. Ruth turned quietly in the bed so as not to disturb Joe, and peered at the luminous figures on the digital clock. Two forty-five. She wanted to slip from beneath the covers and read quietly in the living room until sleep stole up on her. She could see herself, curled on the couch, warm in her cashmere bathrobe, reading—what? She glossed over the title on the book and imagined a nice thick mug of sleep-inducing warm milk, laced with just a touch of whiskey. She was unused to insomnia, a novice at combating it, but she thought the scenario she'd invented as good as any. Why, then, didn't she go for it, as Joe would say?

She clasped her hands together beneath the pillow and tried to relax her body by going limp and unclenching her toes. She breathed deeply, in the correct fashion, tummy in for the outgoing breaths, but that only had the effect of making her self-conscious. It was quiet in the back bedroom, almost eerily so. She and Joe had decided to give the girls the front bedroom, facing on the street, because they agreed that children were oblivious to street noise. It was sometimes disconcerting to look in on Megan and Phoebe, sweetly asleep in their beds with the Laura Ashley canopies, because of the incongruity of the sirens and alarms raging away beyond the windows. Here, in the marital bedroom, Ruth was aware of the minute hum of the digital clock, which gave a little *tack* when, as now, it reached a rounded hour. Three in the morning.

She remembered the actual shock she had felt when she'd first smelled chocolate on her daughters' breath. Phoebe and Megan were allowed candy only on the occasions when they were guests at another child's birthday party. On Halloween, Ruth was accustomed to taking them only to the doors of shareholders who were likeminded and handed over apples or packets of raisins. She had instructed Milagros very carefully, when she'd first arrived, on the girls' diets, stressing that she only wanted Megan and Phoebe to get a "good start" and build sound bones and teeth. Milagros in fact had excellent teeth, and she had imagined her as the product of plantains and fish, or something as wholesome as it was possible to bring to the table in Central America.

"Yes, sure," Milagros had said, nodding vigorously. And she had religiously clung to the late afternoon ritual of scraping carrots and washing celery. The proof of her labors was always to be found in the Adler refrigerator, reposing in Stayfresh baggies.

The thought of the refrigerator made Ruth think of the former President of the Board and, in turn, of Milagros sobbing in Joe's arms, screaming about the dead man's eyes in her primitive and affecting way. Joe had been so good, comforting the hysterical girl, caressing her long, black hair as if she had been Phoebe or Megan crying over a skinned knee. Well, you couldn't blame him for being so solicitous, but a part of Ruth had been revolted by the sight of her small, brown au pair girl clinging so closely to Joe's body and wetting his shirt with her tears.

Had she imagined it, or had Milagros seemed the slightest bit *smug* yesterday, when she told the returning Ruth about Monica's robbery? Murder, robbery, strange figures lurking in the stairwell—these were not features Ruth had factored in when she and Joe had first agreed to buy the apartment. Of course, the apparition on the fire stairs could be discounted, because poor old Mr. Crotty was half-crazed following the death of his wife, as everyone knew. But the rest?

Fay Spooner had told her that Teresa had met a black sociologist loitering near the intercom, trying to determine the racial makeup of the building. Surely such a thing would never have happened if the gutter press hadn't fastened on the ludicrous image of a Robin Hood Murderer! Images of sociologists, intent on milking her building for all it was worth, began to blend with those of Megan and Phoebe greedily biting into huge candy bars while the Adler family dentist sadly shook his head. They were capped by a horrifying dream figure who swung a machete—probably from Honduras—and shattered Monica's window. He was leaping into Monica's bedroom, teeth bared in a hideous grin, when Ruth's eyelids sprang open and revealed the depressing truth. It was now just short of half past three in the morning.

She slid from beneath the ice blue coverings and made her way to the bathroom, where she relieved herself and splashed warm water on her face. She avoided her image in the mirror for the first time. Things were definitely falling apart.

On her way back to bed she considered her earlier plan of the warm milk, but rejected it. The kitchen was too close to Milagros' room. What if the girl heard her, if she wakened and heard the clunk of the saucepan or the kitchen water pipes? She couldn't bear the thought of Milagros lying in the dark, speculating over the presence in the kitchen at an hour when everyone ought to be asleep? And if she actually came out to investigate and encountered her employer in her sleep-shirt pouring whiskey into warm milk, Ruth thought she might die of humiliation.

Just as she had nearly died of humiliation on the one occasion she had tried to broach the subject of her discomfort to Joe.

"I don't think Milagros is a good influence on the girls," she had begun, or words to that effect. She had no doubt sounded pompous, when what she really was feeling was that free-floating anxiety a writer had described in that week's issue of *New York* magazine.

Joe had been all concern at first, but when she had enumerated the complaints against the au pair girl—the chocolate, the apparent disregard of Ruth's wishes—he had simply smiled.

"Lighten up, honey," Joe had said. And then he had gone on to say that *he* found Milagros a definite plus and, while he was all for a balanced diet for Phoebe and Megan, he didn't really believe an occasional candy bar would make them candidates for beriberi. Even at the precise moment Ruth was pondering the expression *Lighten up, honey,* and wondering if it applied to her in general or only in this one matter, he had gone on blithely to deliver a remark so wounding it poisoned Ruth's very existence.

"She's just *young,*" he had said, laughing as if the very idea of the girl's youth gave him pleasure.

Until that moment, Ruth had considered herself young. She was thirty-six, had produced two lovely, albeit female, children, and was soon to go back to a lucrative and demanding job on a full-time basis. What Joe had done in the most casual way was to inform her that the price of all this achievement was the sacrifice of her youth. A true young person now controlled the destinies of her daughters, and Ruth was to "lighten up," and Joe found the impossible Milagros a "plus."

Maternal duty now compelled her to look in on Megan and Phoebe before returning to bed, and even this simple act produced pain. The dim night-light revealed the knitted garments the aunt on St. Nicholas Avenue had lovingly crafted for her niece's charges. They were sweaters. Phoebe's was done in purple wool with scarlet borders, Megan's in the reverse.

The girls adored them and wanted to wear them everywhere.

Beneath the door of every shareholder there appeared a photocopied letter, announcing that the writer had visited the few remaining pawnshops on the West Side, most of them above 100th Street, to try to locate Monica Platt's missing treasures. Since thieves were known to try to "fence" stolen goods, the writer wanted all shareholders to know that he had spared no effort in canvassing possible markets. Working closely with the police had not been a fruitful experience, since the detectives in question had unwisely chosen, in their clannish way, to ignore his seniority and superior experience.

As from this date (read the notice), I shall be working in deepest solitude. Nothing can deter me from my purpose, which is to locate and exterminate the viper who has entered our Garden of Eden.

It was signed, of course, in the name of Timothy Crotty.

TEN

As if to slight the weathermen on the local TV stations, the promised snow blew up to Canada. In late January Columbus Avenue simmered in a sickly heat that would not have been inappropriate in a geriatric hospital room. Women sweated in their fur coats, worn to make the dash to Food World, and the street musicians, seizing the moment, returned. String quartets were heard in the upper reaches of the building, and those who ventured out had to step into the gutters to avoid the throng congregating around the woman who tap-danced on a square of cardboard.

Sarah, her book review completed, stood beneath the building's canopy. It had taken only two days, after all, but she was glad to be outside her apartment, even though the unnatural weather prevented her from taking in deep breaths of fresh, brisk air. As she was contemplating Columbus Avenue with distaste, two strong hands clasped her shoulders with such force she gasped in fear.

"Sarah, sweetie, the very person to accompany me on a walk in the park!" It was Douglas, whom she had not seen since his business trip to Philadelphia.

"You scared me," she said crossly.

"Thought I was the Robin Hood Murderer?" Douglas smiled, revealing his excellent if somewhat wolfish teeth. He was dressed beautifully, as always, and Sarah felt scruffy by comparison. Today he wore a pair of dove gray cotton trousers, topsiders without socks, and a soft old cotton shirt of an even paler gray. A sky blue sweater was knotted casually around his neck. The sweater matched his eyes. "Come, let's walk," he said. "You can fill me in on anything Allen hasn't told me."

"Where is Allen?"

"He's auditioning for a play, something dreary I'm afraid."

Sarah walked at his side a trifle unwillingly. "I hate the park," she said. "Couldn't we go somewhere else?"

"My dear, if you're paying we can fly to Key West, but otherwise it's the park."

On the far side of Columbus a man stood with a saxophone. "I remember him from last summer," Sarah said, "don't you? He's the one who can't actually *play* his instrument, but every now and then he lifts it to his lips and just makes a noise like an elephant trumpeting." And indeed, as if on cue, the man with the saxophone caused it to produce a kind of cosmic farting sound.

"Oh dear," said Douglas. "How extremely depressing."

They walked east one block and then along the perimeter of Central Park until they reached the entrance near Tavern on the Green. Sarah told him what she knew, adding the few small details about Monica's robbery Allen hadn't yet garnered for him. Douglas seemed amused. "Of all the people to rob," he said. "The poor man must have been *livid* when he saw what slim pickings he had to choose from."

They walked past Adventure Playground and crossed to the path running along the meadow. A few daring sun-worshipers had actually removed their shirts, though the temperature could not have been more than sixty. "Looking at some of them," Douglas said, "is not an unalloyed pleasure." He took her arm and guided her firmly away from the path, bounding up a small rise toward some boulders. "One of the nice things about running a small, not very lucrative family business," he said, "is that one's hours are fairly flexible. It's the same with you, dear. As a writer, you have a freedom the office-bound Yuppies would not begin to understand. Try to be grateful."

"Freedom to do what?" Sarah asked ungraciously. "Sit on a pile of stones in Central Park in freak weather?"

"Ah, but think of the company you have." Douglas made such a wry and self-deprecating face that Sarah laughed with genuine surprise. It was true. It was better to be here than in an office, or in her own apartment, where the open windows would admit the flatulent trumpetings of the unmusical saxophonist.

"I have a theory," said Douglas. "Remember, I sat on that Board, so I know Barnett, *knew* him, better than most of you. Not that anyone could ever really *know* the Ice Prince, but you see what I mean. Barnett was a man who believed that he was always, fundamentally and unimpeachably, right. He subscribed to the survival-of-the-fittest doctrine, and he was the fittest of the fit. By his lights, Sarah. He was rich and smart, if unimaginative, and he didn't care what happened to anyone who was less rich or smart than he was. Once, when I ever so mildly remarked that Allen and I would have to leave the building if there were a steep raise in maintenance, he cocked his head, gave me the full attention of those divinely green eyes, and said: 'Then it would be time for you to go, wouldn't it? If you couldn't afford the maintenance, it would mean that you didn't belong here.' "

Yes, that sounded like what she had privately imagined as Barnett Seawright's philosophy. He probably subscribed to the trickle-down theory, too. Sarah lowered her head and pretended to be examining the rather frayed strap of her leather handbag.

"Was he gay, Douglas?" she asked.

"He was, to quote a wit, a screaming heterosexual, Sarah. What would ever make you think otherwise?"

"I thought"—she shrugged to indicate how unimportant her thought had been—"I thought maybe he went in for rough trade? He had a lot of visitors up to the penthouse, and maybe it could have been drugs or something sort of, ah, sexual?"

"Sarah," said Douglas. "You haven't been listening to me. Seawright was a menace, but I don't think he was into drugs or rough trade or kiddie porn or anything remotely close. I touched his hand once by accident, reaching for the ashtray at the board room, and he absolutely *flinched!* I'm sure he had a blood test the next day to see if he'd been contaminated."

"What a disgusting man he was," said Sarah. "I never realized. I suppose anyone who ever had any close contact with him could have wanted to murder him."

"That is precisely my point, dear." Douglas unknotted his sweater and wriggled into it. Two of the last surviving Frisbee players on earth had come into view wearing short shorts and

tank tops. Sarah thought Douglas was making a fashion statement, even if the Frisbee maniacs took no notice.

"But who? Who could he have hurt badly enough to inspire
such a dramatic revenge? Most people aren't capable of doing
what was done to Seawright, no matter how great the provoca-
tion."

Douglas produced a cigarette and lit it, inhaling with the lux-
uriant air of one who is able to smoke so rarely that even the
surgeon general does not place him at risk.

"Monica," he said. "Consider Monica."

If he had not repeated the name, Sarah would have doubted
that she had heard it. She slapped his knee to show that she
didn't take him seriously.

"I don't mean that Monica is the *murderer*, sweetie," said
Douglas. "Monica finds it hard to kill a waterbug. We should
know: Allen and I have had to hold her hand when she installed
mousetraps after the renovations drove the mice up."

"Then what? Why do I have to consider Monica?"

"Because she was robbed," said Douglas. "Someone wanted
something she possessed, and as sure as I'm sitting here it wasn't
her cake plate or her glassware."

Sarah, who shared these views, felt an immense weariness.
She had not expected to defend them on a warm day in January
with granite beneath her bum and an amiable gay man as her
companion. She grunted her agreement.

"How was Monica different from us—you and me?"

Sarah allowed her head to sink to her knee and said, after
careful consideration: "I'm fond of her, Douglas, but she's an
imbecile. We're not."

"Wrong," said Douglas. "Monica is a member of the Board of
Directors, Sarah. We're not."

"So what?"

"Think," said Douglas testily, wrapping his long fingers
round her jaw so she was forced to look at him. "What position
does she fill on the Board?"

"Secretary," said Sarah.

"And what are the Secretary's duties?"

"Take minutes. Send out that silly newsletter."

"Do you have the minutes, sent out from our managing agents, for January?"

"No," said Sarah. "I don't."

"How about the newsletter?"

Sarah tried to remember if there had been a newsletter, sent during the time she had been in London. "I don't think so," she said. Slowly, the import of what Douglas had been saying slid into her consciousness and took hold. There had never been a month when Monica's newsletters had not made their appearance on her doorstep.

"You mean," she said, "that something important happened at the last Board Meeting—something we don't know about?"

Douglas winked, as if to show that she was, after all, a clever girl. Although it was still warm for January, a nasty little wind had sprung up. The sharp, hard-etched buildings of Central Park South rising over the Sheep Meadow, which she had once thought such a beautiful image, were too familiar to move her now. She wondered if those who lived by the sea or high in the mountains also grew indifferent to the beauty around them, but she doubted it. The ceaseless changes of the sea, or of the light as it moved down the mountains, could never become stale, could they? The sight of a lot of overpriced apartment buildings and hotels looming over a meadow whose fences carried signs warning the uninitiated of the presence of rat poison in the grass was another matter.

"I wish the zoo were still open," said Douglas softly.

"I always felt sorry for the animals in that zoo. They were in such exceptionally cramped quarters."

"One always feels sorry for the animals," said Douglas. "But if someone is going to pen them up, one might as well go and visit." He got to his feet and extended a hand to Sarah. "It's probably a good thing they shut it down," he said. "God knows, there's enough animal sacrifice in the park as it is. I can just manage to deal with slaughtered pigeons and chickens, but I'd have to draw the line at camels, say, or seals."

Sarah shot him a startled look. "You sound like Mr. Crotty," she said. "What on earth are you talking about?"

"Religious rites, dear. Strange, voodoolike rituals." He rolled his eyes and made a comic, leering face at her, but she felt chilled all the same. She had always known that a small minority of her fellow New Yorkers practiced religions carried from Africa to the Caribbean, but she had never dreamed that it was a major problem. Walking beside Douglas, she listened as he smugly told her that animal slaughter for religious rituals was up, according to the 20th Precinct, by 60 percent this year. He had asked Dumbrowski, or was it Fields, at any rate the cute black one who *must*, of course, have been Fields since black men were not usually named Dumbrowski, and that was how he knew.

"He must have thought you were—" What? Peculiar? Rude, to single out a black detective and ask him about voodoo?

"I have an inquiring mind," said Douglas. "Nothing wrong with that."

As they passed Adventure Playground Sarah saw, through the denuded trees, the little group of au pairs from her building. While the children staggered about in the sand, shrieking and pushing one another, their minders stood at the edge of the open pit, deep in conversation.

"Milagros is back," observed Sarah. "Poor kid."

"Lucky that Seawright has gone to his reward. He *hated* her. He was not too pleased at the presence of the West Indian girls, but he really had it in for Milagros."

"Why? Just because she's brown?"

Douglas frowned. "Not that simple," he said. At that moment the Irish girl looked up and saw them. She waved a hand in greeting, smiling beneath her marmalade-colored spikes of hair. Jewel and Norrie waved, more laconically, and when Milagros spotted Douglas she lifted a hand, too. They looked, Sarah thought, like a poster commissioned by the United Nations.

Douglas seemed deep in thought. It wasn't until they were passing the rank of limousines parked at Tavern on the Green that he readdressed himself to Seawright's dislike of the girl from Honduras. "I don't think Barnett was your conventional bigot," he said. "He was a class bigot, or what he thought of as class. I'm sure he'd be proud to know a black man who was a successful stockbroker, or a Puerto Rican corporate raider.

They'd rank higher in the Seawright view than a white cop or short-order cook."

"How about a black bishop?" Sarah asked, thinking of Desmond Tutu, who had entered her apartment recently, through the miracle of television, to suggest that the President of the United States was somewhat insincere in his opposition to apartheid.

"You must be joking."

"I was."

They passed a derelict sleeping on a bench. The man's body was mercifully covered by a garment so discolored and stiffened that it was impossible to know what it had once been, but his bare feet protruded from the bundle, and they were ulcerated and possibly gangrenous. Sarah forced herself to dwell on the man's feet, then turned to her companion and asked:

"Well, what the hell do you expect me to do?"

"Submit your name as a candidate," replied Douglas immediately. "For the Board of Directors."

"You couldn't stick it—why should I?"

Douglas appeared to turn the question over in his mind, but she felt quite sure he was playacting. She wanted to clutch his arm, draw him to a bench, but they kept on walking, leaving the park and the limousines, the sleeping derelict and the au pairs, the shopworn view of the Essex House and the Plaza, even the last Frisbee players in the Western World.

"Because," said Douglas in a remote and snooty way, "because you're healthy and I'm not. Got it?"

And so she understood that her handsome and imperious neighbor had probably received the news, and was dying.

Monica was feeling very much abandoned. The police who had been sent to investigate her robbery didn't seem interested, not really. She recognized Tim Crotty as an ally, but that was to be expected. She had known Tim for so many years she didn't care to count them up. Monica was by nature optimistic, but the horrible events in her building had made her question the nature of her credo, and this spiritual inventory had plunged her into a state of what she thought of as despair.

Really, what she didn't want was to equate Tim Crotty with herself. They had both lost their life's partners—and wasn't that a lovely phrase?—but whereas Tim had always been dependent on Kitty, she, Monica, had never relied on Otto to give her the cachet, the *prominence*, she had always felt to be hers. Monica knew she was special, but she had never tried to emphasize it. She prided herself on her ability to assume the "common touch," and wondered why more shareholders hadn't lauded her efforts at bridging the gap.

Her newsy little recounting of the Board meetings, for example. Her newsletters, typed, Xeroxed, and lovingly placed under the door of each shareholder. It wasn't easy for her, now that she was getting on, to cover each of the building's nine floors, and often the elevator didn't wait and she had to walk up a flight. Why hadn't anyone expressed appreciation for her dedication? Of course it was her job, as Secretary, to take the minutes, but the newsletter was something special, an extra. She always used it as an opportunity for welcoming new shareholders to the building, bidding farewell to those departing, welcoming newborn infants, or congratulating neighbors on some achievement. It was so much nicer than a straightforward description of the dreary work proceeding on the roof or in the basement, together with the sum of money the Board had approved for the hiring of various contractors, so much more *neighborly* than a bald recital of electrical problems and water pressure complaints.

She felt she had put more into the building than the building was giving back. Ever since her robbery she almost felt the building was hostile toward her—not, in fact, her neighbors, but the building itself. She knew this was an irrational feeling, but the sight of her pillaged bedroom had changed her in a way she thought was probably permanent. She would never again turn her key in the lock without a small tightening in her stomach, and she would never approach her bedroom without fearing a sudden blast of cold air, as from a shattered window. She and Otto had been robbed twice in the thirty-two years of their marriage—she wasn't *that* sheltered—but it was much more unsettling when you were alone.

Alone. Monica hated the word, and hated even more applying it to herself. She had lots of good friends, Ida Strabinski here in the building and chums from her working years, when she had contributed to the Platt budget by taking scores of temporary office jobs. She was free to lift the telephone and call any one of them and set up an evening at the movies, or a free concert at the church two blocks away, but something prevented her. It all went back to the newsletter, the nagging thought that wouldn't quite come clear. Until she got it straight, she was unable to attend to other things.

She sat in her living room, forcing herself to concentrate. Several days had passed between the last Board meeting and the murder of Barnett Seawright. She had not seen him in that little space, but she had talked to him. He had called to tell her not to distribute the newsletter, as usual, and she had felt bewildered, then humiliated. Apparently someone had complained about her syntax, her grammar. She didn't know who it had been, but Ed Knowles had mentioned once, in passing, that Monica might do well to proofread her efforts more carefully before taking them to be duplicated. What had she said to that cold, confident voice on the telephone?

"I can assure you, Barnett, that I have taken scruples with this latest newsletter." Something like that. Surprisingly, he had laughed. "No, Monica, it's not a question of proofreading," he had said. "Just hold on to it until I can get back to you. I have to check some figures. I'm sorry you've written it already, because I think it will have to be totally redone."

He hadn't sounded sorry at all, had even seemed to take pleasure in the words *totally redone*. Still, she was so relieved that no personal criticism was winging her way it did not occur to her to feel resentful. But something strange—he had made her promise to obey him, as if they were discussing something more important than the newsletter. "Yes, I promise, yes of course," she'd stammered to this man who was young enough to be her son. And then a few days later, he was dead. She would never know, now, why he had made his strange request.

Only this morning one of the new shareholders had called to her: "Where's the newsletter?" She would hate to be thought a derelict, as it were, in her duties. She supposed she could call Ed Knowles, or the managing agent, to see if the figures in question had been dug up. Smiling, pleased at the idea of something to do, Monica caressed the Royal Doulton milkmaid figurine on her just-so coffee table. Then she went to her bedroom to get the original newsletter, so she could make the changes before settling down to rewrite it. The window had been fixed and the room was warm and unthreatening, and Monica began to think that she would not, after all, be obliged to feel differently about it. "A place for everything and everything in its place," she said aloud. The box of tissues was in its fluffy blue cosy, chosen to match the doorknob covers and bathroom carpeting. Her address book was neatly centered on the bedside table, its pencil for jotting notes magnetized to the cover. Her original copies of her newsletters were in a mauve folder in the drawer of the table, neatly and chronologically stacked. She hummed as she withdrew the topmost sheet of paper and began to read her own cheerful prose. She hadn't read very far before she knew she had the wrong document, and the date at the top and the scrolled *Happy Holidays* at the bottom confirmed it. This was the December newsletter. She spread the mauve folder open and went through every paper inside, thinking she must have thrust it in at random, but it was no use. The January newsletter was simply not there. It had vanished.

She began to feel even more melancholy as she realized that everything was not in its place, after all.

ELEVEN

Sarah opened her door to a wholesome-looking blond woman whose pale hair swung about her face like a perfect bell. She seemed to be in her late twenties and was simply but expensively dressed. There was something puzzlingly familiar about her, and as she offered a tentative smile Sarah could almost make a connection.

"Hello," the woman said. "May I come in for a moment? I'm Suzy Seawright."

Of course. She had her brother's green eyes, but eyes which in the male had carried a polar chill were, in the female, simply pretty green eyes. "Barney's sister," she explained.

Sarah asked her to come in, privately marveling that anyone, even his sister, had called the dead man "Barney." She could imagine all too well what Suzy Seawright was doing in New York; what she could not understand was why she was being visited by her. She said the conventional thing: "I'm awfully sorry about your brother, Ms. Seawright. I'm afraid I didn't know him very well."

"Suzy. Please call me Suzy." She was wearing what looked like a cashmere dress to Sarah, who had not for a long time worn anything so nice, at least during the day. It was of a pale rosy shade, and was belted at Suzy's slender waist. Her boots and purse were of plain, good black leather, and she was carrying her coat over her arm, as if she had spent some time in the building before coming to Sarah. She sat in the big leather armchair which had once belonged to Sarah's husband, and which he had never claimed.

"I'm sure you can't imagine why I'm here," she said.

"Well, I suppose it has something to do with your brother," said Sarah, feeling as if she were on a stage set. She wondered if she ought to offer Suzy Seawright a drink, but before she could do so her visitor spoke again.

"You said you didn't know Barney well. That's not unusual, not at all. I would have been very surprised if you had said anything else. *I* didn't know him very well, at least after we'd both grown up. You could say that my brother didn't encourage —attachments. I'm sure you found him cold, a trifle removed?"

"Yes. A trifle removed is a good way of putting it, but then, I didn't think he should have to be terribly warm to me. We met only in the elevator, or the lobby. He was always polite, and that's all I require of my neighbors."

Suzy nodded and smiled delightedly, as if some point had been proven. "Now I know why he liked you," she said. "You are just as practical and honest as he said you were."

Sarah was as amazed as she would have been if her caller had hitched up her rosy dress and executed a cartwheel on the living room carpet. "Barnett—*liked* me? Liked *me?*"

"In his fashion," said Suzy, "I think he did."

"Well forgive me," said Sarah, lighting a cigarette with suddenly trembling fingers, "but if your brother liked me, Ms. Seawright, Suzy, it comes as a complete and stunning surprise. He never showed any signs of it."

"He wouldn't, of course. He'd respect your privacy that much more, because in some way he admired you. When Barney liked people, he tried to leave them alone."

It was growing dark and a wintry twilight, belying the earlier warm spell, had crept into the room. Sarah felt she ought to turn on a lamp but was too enervated to do so. It had been a long time since she had been so surprised by anything another human being had said to her. At last she cleared her throat and asked: "How do you know that your brother had any feelings of —esteem, shall we say—for me? Couldn't you be confusing me with someone else?"

"Oh, no," said Suzy, in her soft and childish voice. "He told me that Sarah Mason, that's you, isn't it, was one of the few people in his co-op who didn't make him want to scream with impatience. He said that on the telephone to me just a few months ago. He'd read a piece you'd written for the *Times* maga-

zine section, and he said it summed up his own feelings about
divorce in the proverbial nutshell. That's when he called you
practical and honest. Those were words of high praise for my
brother."

Sarah remembered the article well. It had been a skittish piece
of work, brittle and rather arch. It had grown out of her dislike
for the spate of earnest writings which professed to find divorce
an experience so shattering as to render its victims emotional
cripples. She had argued that divorce was now so common, so
much the norm, that to treat the children of divorce with the
same solemnity one might treat children in Cambodia or Ethio-
pia was morally repellent. She still believed it was true, but
would willingly have recalled the piece if it had been within her
power. For one thing, she had been too cavalier. For another,
she had no children herself, and was not the proper commenta-
tor.

"You see," said Suzy, "I was one of the people Barney was
fond of. That's why he called me occasionally. Never on my
birthday, or at Christmas, because that would have been sentimental. He called me maybe twice a year, at odd times, and he
always discussed his neighbors, wherever he was living."

"Where did he live before he came here?"

"Always in New York," said Suzy. "There were at least four
or five apartments he lived in here. All co-ops."

Sarah ground out her cigarette, immediately longing for another, if only to occupy her hands. "And was he always on the
Board of Directors in those co-ops?" she said, striving for the
manner of a panelist on a General Knowledge quiz show.

"Yes," said Suzy Seawright. "That's how Barney got so rich,
you know. He'd buy a place and do it up, then sell it. It was
what he called his formula. He said there would never be a time
like this again, and he would be crazy not to take advantage. He
always got himself elected to the Board of Directors—that way
he could make policy, as he called it, something to do with the
bylaws—to protect his investment."

So, Barnett had been a privateer, a pirate. It didn't surprise
her at all. In the past, when he was new and the subject of the
building's gossip, it had been rumored that he had a large pri-

vate income. Sarah roused herself, turned on the lamp, and asked her guest if she would like a drink. Suzy declined, and then went on with her topic doggedly.

"Barnett did go to law school," she said, "and he did work in a firm back home for a while, but then our father died in a plane crash and Barney took his share of what we inherited and cleared off to New York."

"And what did you do with yours?" asked Sarah gently. She was horrified the moment the words were out of her mouth. This young woman wasn't the subject of an interview, after all. She began to apologize, but Suzy didn't seem to expect an apology.

"I didn't really need mine," she said. "I'd just married and moved to Grosse Pointe when poor Dad died. My husband is one of the richest men in the Midwest." Suzy giggled with delight. "I don't often get to say that, but I thought you wouldn't mind."

Sarah thought that Suzy enjoyed her wealth in a comparatively innocent manner; she was like a little girl rejoicing in a shiny doll carriage. Unlike her brother, she had not allowed herself to believe that she had joined an aristocracy of some sort. Her life may have become gentrified, but she would not think of herself as one of the gentry.

"I called myself Suzy Seawright to make it easier for you to understand who I was," she said, looking amused.

"But Seawright is your maiden name," Sarah said. "Anyone would have done it, under the circumstances."

"Not exactly, I'm afraid. Barney chose 'Seawright' for himself after he came to New York. He liked the way it sounded. He made it legal, too, changed it by deed poll or whatever you call it."

"What was his real name?"

"Jensen," said Suzy, laughing out loud.

"Barnett Jensen," said Sarah, trying it on her tongue. At this Suzy laughed harder. "No," she sputtered. "The Barnett part was his middle name, our mom's name before she was married. He was called Fred. Fred B. Jensen. Barnett was too much for me when I'd known him all my life as Fred, so I had to shorten it to Barney."

"He must have hated that," said Sarah.

"Oh, I never called him that to his *face*. Only when I was talking to the police back when he was first—" She stopped smiling. "When he died. And now again, when I came to see you."

Mention of her brother's death subdued her now, and Sarah wondered if she really felt it so keenly or was only appalled at her recent hilarity over his pretensions. She wanted to know many things, among them whether he had been buried beneath a headstone as Fred or Barnett, but she could scarcely ask.

"We had him cremated, back in Minneapolis," Suzy said, as if reading her mind. "I came back after the will was read, because of the penthouse. It's sealed off, you know, but I had to get an evaluation, for the estate. The money will be held in trust for his daughter until she's twenty-one. She's only nine now."

"I didn't realize he'd been married," said Sarah. "Is his widow a Mrs. Seawright or a Mrs. Jensen?"

"Oh, she's a Jensen all right," said Suzy briskly. "That marriage only lasted eighteen months, and my niece is the only good thing that came out of it. Holly's a darling."

"One of the few he was fond of?"

"He barely knew her," said Suzy. "I think Fred hated children, only he didn't realize how much until after she was born. It's weird, when you think of it, because he left everything to her. Maybe there was something good in him after all?"

Sarah looked at the former Suzy Jensen who, by virtue of her prettiness and sweet nature, had become the wife of one of the richest men in the Midwest, and tried to frame her words carefully, to offer some small crumb of comfort which Suzy could take away and reexamine at a later time, but in the end she could only offer a cliché.

"There were probably many good things about him, Suzy," she said, not believing it for a moment. "People are mysteries."

Privately, she knew exactly why Fred B. Jensen had left his riches to the daughter he had not bothered to know. When it came right down to it, he could only bear to share his spoils with someone who was a part of himself, and even then, only after death.

Mr. Crotty had never before stayed on at O'Reilly's for more than an hour, or so he persuaded himself. He purposefully ignored the times when he had consulted his watch and discovered that the late afternoon had mysteriously vanished and been replaced by the early evening. There were many good reasons to limit his time at O'Reilly's, not the least being his finances. He liked a Guinness, or two, but you could hardly make two pints last for more than two hours. Another reason was his deep desire to maintain a sort of structure in his life. Kitty had always had dinner on the table at six-thirty, and there'd been hell to pay if a fella was late. Now that he was under no timetable of tyranny, he found that he missed it. The only people who sat in a neighborhood bar at dinnertime were people who had no place else to go.

O'Reilly's was the last bar left on Columbus Avenue that didn't make him feel like an anachronism. All the old places had shut down to make room for those restaurants that served raw fish, or for boutiques that sold yachting clothes. Either that, or they'd been smartened up and turned into watering holes for the television people. The Shamrock, which had once very much resembled O'Reilly's, was now a place where you might see the anchorman of Mr. Crotty's favorite network news program bellying up to the bar, and that was an alarming turn of events.

Tonight had been a special occasion, because he'd met the youngish nephew of Patsy the barman, and J.J. had turned out to be—like Mr. Crotty—a philatelist. Stamps were his passion. J.J. appreciated both their beauty and their historic value. It was rare to encounter a younger person who really cared for stamps, still rarer to find one who was impressed by his own intimate knowledge of the inner workings of the Colonus Stamp Company, in whose service he had labored, as second-in-charge, right up until his retirement.

J.J. was over on a visit from Ireland, and he had entered the long, dusty corridor of O'Reilly's only to give his uncle a message. How had the subject of stamps been introduced? Never mind, not important. The boy had insisted on buying shots of Irish to go with the Guinness, and time had oiled by on the twin treads of drink and an interested audience. Mr. Crotty had positively bloomed, his tongue set free to praise or condemn the latest commemoratives. He remembered delivering a long speech about the possible mistakes the Australians might make in the design of their bicentennial, and it was when he was recounting the antics of an eccentric Englishman who had purchased an uninhabitable island in the North Sea in order to issue a stamp bearing his image . . . That was when he had detected boredom in young J.J.'s eyes. Time to cut his losses and go home.

Mr. Crotty looked round and saw that O'Reilly's clientele had changed. J.J. had disappeared, and he was surrounded by a downscale version of the very people who had displaced him at The Shamrock. They were all young enough to be his children. They were packing in, settling in the fake leather booths, thronging around the bar, removing jackets, unwinding long scarves. Even the bartender had left, and had been replaced by a young man with a mustache. Feeling caught in the grip of a waking dream, Mr. Crotty got down from his stool and backed away through the crowd. Above the bar the clock with the shamrocks instead of numbers seemed to be telling him that it was now ten-thirty. "Impossible," he said aloud, and a young woman in a Mets T-shirt heard him and giggled.

Outside on the pavement he checked his watch. That business of having shamrocks instead of numerals was confusing, and he hoped he had misread the clock, but no, it was actually ten thirty-two.

The Avenue was swarming with figures, all wearing those silly big coats, now that the warm spell had broken. He could see them filling the raw fish restaurant, spilling out almost into the street at Raider's Wine Bar. He headed north for half a block, keeping to the walls of the darkened Food World, hoping his gait was that of a sober man. There were disturbing rumors afoot that Food World might be closing down to make room for a huge clothing store, and if Food World went, then surely

O'Reilly's could not last much longer, despite its thriving appearance?

Mr. Crotty crossed over into his own street, wondering if he should take a bracing walk around the block once or twice to clear his head. On the other hand, he hadn't eaten since noon, and he knew he should put something in a stomach which currently contained large amounts of Guinness and Irish. He fumbled for his keys, hoping he would meet no neighbor tonight.

Luck was with him. There was no one waiting for the elevator or lurking in the lobby. Automatically, he glanced at the brass letter boxes to see if Ernesto and the new porter were on the job, polishing and shining all the lobby paraphernalia that had cost an arm and a leg. Everything seemed to be in order. He rode to the ninth floor in a mood of euphoria, now that he had returned home unnoticed. In his kitchen he heated up a tin of tomato soup and slapped slices of packaged ham between two pieces of white bread. All of these purchases had been made at Food World, and he wondered, screwing open the little jar of French's Mustard, where he would shop if it closed down. He had visited the fancy new emporium on Broadway, and he thought he remembered that they didn't even *have* his brand of mustard. There had been exotic brown mustards, and ones with wine and shallots and foreign bodies in them, but no reassuring, primary-yellow mustards a fella with plain eating habits could stomach.

He spent so much time reflecting on what the closure of Food World would do to his daily routine that the tomato soup came to a violent boil and gave forth an unpleasant, scorched odor. He tipped the soup into the sink and ran water into the saucepan. He found that he had little appetite for the ham sandwich, but forced himself to take three bites, chewing mechanically. He had found that he was unable to duplicate the specific tastes Kitty had manufactured for him in the years of their marriage, and wondered what she would have put into the ham sandwich to make it palatable.

Leaving the uneaten sandwich in the kitchen, Mr. Crotty sauntered into his living room and told himself he was going to stand by the window and look out at the night. He did not acknowledge his detour to the sideboard, where he poured an inch of whiskey into his usual glass, any more than he took conscious note of the fact that the glass had not been washed since the night before. The straightforward view from his window was so depressing he usually angled his body uncomfortably against the wall and stared eastward, where a sliver of glamorous New York skyline could be glimpsed. He had pointed the view out to Martin, his son, when Martin had bought the apartment for his parents as an investment. "You can see the San Remo," he had said. "Christ, Dad," Martin had countered, "not without being a contortionist."

"Things seem to be coming apart," said Mr. Crotty, once more speaking aloud, and not too eager to investigate the meaning of the words once he'd heard them. It wasn't his way to be self-pitying, and he squared his shoulders and decided it was time for Vertical Patrol. Despite the police department's lack of encouragement, Mr. Crotty had been on the job ever since he'd announced his intentions in the lobby. His word was not to be taken lightly. On this very day he had wandered the back stairs twice: once at 9:00 A.M. and then again just before he had gone off to O'Reilly's for his afternoon jaunt.

The Samoan war club was where he had left it, leaning against the umbrella stand in the hall. It had been a gift from Lyman Coates, the much-traveled President of the Colonus Stamp Company, and made a fine protective weapon. He hefted it like a batter about to go to the plate and let himself out into the hallway. It was now nearly eleven-thirty, and the building, on this weekday night, was peaceful and silent at its center. He walked up the steps to the region of the penthouses, peering about for any sign of an intruder. Then he walked back down, patrolling the stairs with his war club, a benevolent figure, intent on keeping his neighbors safe from further violence.

At the seventh-floor landing he saw that someone had violated the rules and placed a pizza box near the service elevator for collection. "Mustn't be a stickler, but it could conceivably cause a vermin problem," he muttered, as if to an associate who was taping his observances. At the sixth floor he was reminded of poor dear Monica's terrible experience. He thought he should write Monica a little note, but he didn't want her to misinterpret his motives.

At the fifth, something penetrated unpleasantly, causing him to stand stock-still and sniff the air. There was a definite odor, alien and not natural to the premises. He thought it was the smell of old potato sacks, which was not in itself alarming, but it prompted a memory. On one of his walks he had passed an old man dressed in a soiled raincoat, his face so begrimed that it was impossible to tell his natural color. He had been weaving about on a traffic island near Broadway, and a sudden wind had parted the flaps of his coat to reveal that he was quite naked beneath, except for a furry garment Mr. Crotty could only think of as a loincloth. The man's spindly, undernourished legs had appeared as something obscene, but he had tried to cover his private parts in fur, and Mr. Crotty remembered all too well how he had tried to puzzle it out—where had the sad, homeless man acquired the scrap of fur with which to safeguard his decency? At any rate, he had smelled suspiciously like the smell settling over the fifth floor.

Lifting the war club to battle position, Mr. Crotty rounded the corner and approached the fire stairs. The door had been firmly closed, and the frosted window revealed no silhouette. He opened the door and grunted with surprise to find what he had been looking for and never really expected to find. The dark figure was real, and it huddled against the far wall, arms stiffly held to its sides, face cast down, like a guilty and penitent schoolboy. The smell was overpowering now, and Mr. Crotty wished he had remembered to bring his police whistle.

He shouted at the cowering figure, asking it what it was doing on the fire stairs, but there was no answer. Feeling frozen in a nightmare ten times more potent than the one he had experienced at O'Reilly's, Mr. Crotty began to speak of citizen's arrests, of murder and robbery and mayhem, of law and order and the need for a decent society to play by the rules, but none of it moved the man he thought of as his captive.

At last he grasped the apparition's arm, thinking to lead him out of the fire stairs, but his contact with the intruder's flesh produced astonishing results. The slight form which had sought to make itself invisible now bucked frantically in an effort to lose the offending arm, for all the world as if it were an unbroken horse Mr. Crotty had tried to mount. A thin, wailing noise came from the creature's mouth, a sound which distressed Mr. Crotty so much he dropped the war club and covered his ears. The clatter of hardwood on the tiles silenced the intruder, who backed further into the dim passage and stared at the fallen weapon.

Thinking that he would be able to reason with the pathetic man, Mr. Crotty bent to retrieve Lyman Coates' gift. It was the wrong thing to do. Surprisingly strong hands closed over his own, fighting for possession of the war club, and Mr. Crotty was the loser. One blow was all that was needed to shatter his skull, and he went hurtling down the stairs, his problems about where to shop and when to drink ended forever.

TWELVE

It was Ernesto who found Mr. Crotty's body the next day, during his routine check of the fire stairs. They only opened on the outside on the higher floors, and he had noticed that the door on the fifth was slightly ajar. Peering inside, he could see nothing unusual on the landing, but there was something which compelled him to enter the little space. It was the trace of a smell he knew all too well, and it lingered on the fire stairs, faint but persistent. It was, Ernesto thought, the smell of a homeless one. It went beyond the odor of normal, unwashed bodies at the end of a long day's work: it suggested a dry rot and decay.

He looked down the stairwell and drew in his breath on a sharp, hissing note. There was a large dark shape in the dimness, and even before he'd gone halfway down to the landing below he could see it was the Señor Crotty. He lay on his back, and the force of the fall must have jackknifed him so that his head was propped up against the wall at an odd angle. His legs and feet lay on the bottom stairs, and on his face was a look Ernesto thought inappropriate in a dead man: Mr. Crotty looked *disappointed.* Here were no nightmare, staring eyes of the kind that had sent Milagros shrieking up to St. Nicholas Avenue. The old man's eyes were at half-mast, his mouth was drawn downward. Ernesto thought he could see what had happened. Mr. Crotty had had too much to drink—Ernesto had often smelled drink on his breath in these past few months—and he had ventured forth in the night in his crazy plan of helping the police and blundered down the fire stairs to his death.

It was a shame, really, because he had been a good man. Ernesto had told Milagros that Señor Crotty was crazy only for something to say, and also, to be truthful, because on that very day the old one had pestered him about shining the brass in the lobby. Ernesto said a prayer for Mr. Crotty's soul and then sprinted up the fire stairs and into the service elevator. In his apartment in the courtyard he had a card with the names of the two cops who had come when Seawright's body was found. There was a number where they could be reached at any time, and Ernesto wondered whether to use it, since the death in the stairwell had been an accidental one.

He was already rehearsing his answer to the inevitable question about why he had happened to peer down the little-used stairs. The smell was not something he wished to mention, because it opened a line of questioning that could have unpleasant repercussions. He had convinced himself that the smell was an illusion, a divine magic trick perpetrated so that he would make the discovery before the unfortunate Crotty began to decompose and send up a smell much more disturbing.

He slid the moving grille open with a satisfying clash, and was in the act of crossing the lobby to the stairs leading to his quarters when a voice rang out:

"Ernesto, I'm so glad I've found you! Could you possibly make time to come up to my apartment and look at the toilet in the maid's room?" Mrs. Spooner was sitting on the edge of the radiators, sorting her mail.

"Maybe later," he said. "Later this afternoon, OK?"

"So much junk mail," said Mrs. Spooner vaguely. "Where does it all come from, Ernesto?"

He laughed, insincerely, and pivoted on his heel. Mrs. Spooner was exactly the kind of tenant who would make it her business to see that Ernesto was out of a job if she ever *knew*. She belonged with the new crowd, who wanted a round-the-clock doorman. Spooners, Adlers, Knowleses, and the dead Seawright all agreed that their properties would be worth much more if they could boast a doorman. So would whoever bought the two apartments sudden death had rendered empty.

If any of the doorman crew even suspected that Ernesto had been alerted to Mr. Crotty's tragic end on account of the strange smell, his job would be terminated with a ruthless and unarguable swiftness.

The first one had been an old woman he'd found sleeping in

the outer lobby at six in the morning. She was making a pillow of her shopping bags, both for comfort and to protect the objects inside them. She was white, this unfortunate, and when he'd roused her and told her she must go, she had turned on him her pale blue eyes and cursed at him. Then, as an afterthought, she had said, "It was raining."

How did they get into the building? The man with the dirty raincoat he had discovered last November, after a three-day spell of bitter weather? The man was so shrunken that Ernesto had at first thought him a heap of rags mysteriously deposited at the entrance. "It looked like snow," the man had whispered before closing the tails of his coat and casting about for his few possessions. One of them had been a half-smoked cigarette butt. "It looked like snow," he had repeated, before he gathered his ruined limbs together and stumbled out through the new mahogany doors the co-op had recently installed.

Ernesto, poised at the telephone, no longer knew where his loyalties lay. In the old days he would have ordered any bum out of his clean, polished lobby without hesitation, perhaps with a sense of outrage. The idea of any of the tenants stumbling over a derelict on *his* preserve would have been the first thought to cross his mind. In the old days, too, he had tended to think of the few bums and street people he saw as strange creatures who had renounced normal living and preferred their independence. And, in fact, not a one of them had ever sought shelter in his building. Not until the neighborhood had begun to change.

It was mystifying. You saw these derelict people all the time, now; the streets were thick with them, ambling along with no purpose, sleeping over warm-air grates, occasionally sitting on the pavement in front of restaurants howling. You called them "The Homeless," and you did so not because they were any more homeless than the bums of seven years ago, but because there were so many of them. Ernesto had once thought of himself as a Puerto Rican, whereas now he and his countrymen were "Hispanics," just as the bums and bag ladies were now The Homeless, and the former tenants of his building had become Shareholders.

He dialed 911 and was put on hold, then handed over to a

voice he recognized as Hispanic. Nevertheless, he spoke in English, identifying himself and his building, and explaining that a man was dead on the fire stairs. The voice informed him that 911 was a number to call for ongoing crimes, and if the individual were dead he might wish to phone Roosevelt Hospital or the 20th Precinct.

He chose the precinct house, since a hospital was not going to do poor Crotty any good, and repeated his information.

He knew that he would deny it if anyone asked him if he had ever spotted intruders in the building. It couldn't matter, since the old man had clearly fallen down the stairs on his own, and how could he explain—particularly in English—how he would feel if asked to evict a homeless one from the premises on a freezing night in January? He had never thought, back when he had first assumed his duties as a super, that they would one day empower him to pass a death sentence.

By midafternoon the detectives from Homicide North were once more trudging from apartment to apartment, asking their seemingly pointless questions. They were treating Mr. Crotty's abrupt end as accidental death, they told everyone, but in an unsolved homicide a death in the same building merited close scrutiny.

In Monica's ornate living room they met with a strange turn: Monica was feeling genuine grief at Tim's terrible departure from her world, but she was unable to suppress another, less worthy emotion. Why hadn't Dumbrowski and Fields come when she'd been robbed? Surely it was all part and parcel of the same crime wave?

Joe Dumbrowski wondered why the pretentious old bird equated homicide, break-and-enter, and accidental death and came up with a seamless whole, but Roland Fields came away with something more interesting. Mrs. Platt had a secret which she was dying to tell, but something was holding her back. Something was more frightening to Mrs. Platt than withholding information from the police. Probably it was a small, boring secret of no account, but it existed, and at some future date he would find it out. The murder of Barnett Seawright was the first he had encountered that sometimes seemed unsolvable, and he knew the reason.

No matter how lacking in social contacts a murder victim was, there was always somebody who cared. An old mama, a priest or pastor who had held some hope for the immortal soul of a seriously disjointed member of his flock, a bed partner, or long-lost relative, or vendor who remembered the corpse as a faithful customer. Always someone. Even the expendable bums who were sometimes incinerated in Lower East Side parks or in the homeless dormitories pitched in the old train yards by the Hudson River. They had all left their marks, their proofs of having been alive at some time, and there was always someone who came forward to make the necessary connection.

"The poor old dear," said Douglas to the police. "He was missing his wife, and he took to the drink, and that was that. He had these grandiose *illusions* about keeping the building safe, and look where it landed him. So much for illusions."

"The fag put on a real show," observed Joe Dumbrowski. "Delicate tears and everything."

Roland, who knew the tears were real, said nothing.

"Mr. Crotty always seemed unbalanced," said Mrs. Adler. "Salt of the earth, of course, but a bit of a tippler."

"I didn't really know the man," Mrs. Spooner confided, in the manner of one who had never tried an inferior brand. "But he did maintain he'd seen someone lurking about at night. Surely this is proof that this building needs twenty-four-hour protection? Wouldn't you say, speaking professionally, that it has become a necessity?"

Maryanne Francini was vaguely hostile, instructing the two, by her tone of voice, in what they could and could not reasonably expect her to answer. "No, I didn't see him at all yesterday. If I had I would tell you, but whether or not poor Mr. Crotty drank too much is his business and no one else's."

Sarah was marginally more helpful, revealing that she had seen Mr. Crotty go into O'Reilly's at some time the previous afternoon.

Martin Crotty, the dead man's son, had been notified and was expected to meet the detectives at five. He would be driving in from Pearl River. It would be a long time before they'd leave the building that evening, considering all the apartments they'd have to revisit to interview husbands and others not at home in the afternoon, and there would be no pathology report until the next day, after Martin had formally identified the body. Dumbrowski and Fields took the opportunity to pay a call on O'Reilly's barman, Pat McCann.

"Ah, Jesus, what a hell of a thing," McCann said when Roland explained the nature of their visit. He confirmed that Mr. Crotty had come in at his usual time, about four in the afternoon, but when asked if Crotty had been a heavy drinker he laughed, then fiddled with the tap and looked mournful, remembering that his old client's drinking habits were a thing of the past. "Not a'tall," he said. "Many's the time he'd nurse a pint for an hour. I expect he was on a tight budget, and came in more for the company than the drink. I'd slip him one on the house when I could."

"Then if he was intoxicated last night," asked Roland politely, "he didn't get that way here?"

McCann's face took on a shifty look, and Roland could almost hear him calculating his answer. Had the time really arrived when barmen could be held responsible for fatal accidents suffered after a patron had left? Crotty wasn't driving, after all. "To tell the truth," he said, "he was still here last night after I went off duty at eight. It was the only time it had ever happened. My nephew from Ireland came in and struck up a conversation with Tim. Bought him some shots, too. You'd have to ask the night man when he actually left."

Long before the pathologist's report was made known, Roland refused to accept Mr. Crotty's death as an accident. No matter how smoothly everything conspired to point in that direction—and the fact that Mr. Crotty seemed to have tied one on at O'Reilly's during his last night on earth furthered the accident theory—Roland smelled a rat. Crotty would almost surely have had to fall down the stairs backward to land in the position he'd been in, and even an inebriated man would not have entered the fire stairs and examined the wall rather than the staircase. If Mr. Crotty had lost his balance and plunged down the stairs, wouldn't he have landed face down? Even if his body had somersaulted, it would have been prevented by its own weight from landing face up and legs spread over the bottom stairs—a position more likely if he had been shoved and propelled backward. If he had been confronting someone on the dim landing, he might have stood with his back to the stairs, mightn't he?

Then, too, Fields had seen many drunks who had fallen down stairs, and the only one who had died had been a very old and fragile woman, and even she had not died then and there, but three days later at the hospital. Broken legs and arms and ribs were more likely. He had not told Dumbrowski any of his theories. He knew Joe wanted Mr. Crotty's death to be exactly what it appeared to be, and until more potent evidence emerged, in the shape of a lab report, he was content to keep silent.

When they returned to the building to keep their appointment with Martin Crotty, they encountered a tall, reedy man with a face so pale Fields wondered if his pallor was due to shock, grief, guilt, or a combination of all three. He did not suspect the junior Crotty of any crime, but he did imagine Martin might be suffering guilt for another reason. He was right, for almost the first thing the man said when they had ridden up to the ninth floor was: "I always intended to visit him more often. Especially now that—my mother died earlier this year, you know. Maybe if I'd visited on a more regular basis . . ."

Martin Crotty inserted his key—he was, after all, the actual owner of the apartment in which his parents had lived—and let them into the dim vestibule of the apartment where he had grown up. No light burned in the living room, but the overhead was on in the kitchen, showing the remains of a ham sandwich on the oilcloth-covered kitchen table. Several dirty saucepans were lined up on the old-fashioned stove, and a gelatinous mass of red partly spackled the sink. Soup, not blood, thought Fields. The forensics men had presumably combed the fire stairs, and he and Joe were simply having a look at the deceased's apartment.

"The last supper," said Dumbrowski, pointing to the half-eaten ham sandwich, lowering his voice so only Roland would hear his witticism.

Martin trailed them through the apartment, down the hall, and into the messy rooms. One contained only cartons and books, stacked neatly enough but in need of a dusting.

"This used to be my bedroom," said Martin.

Back in the living room, lights were turned on and a cursory examination made. On a sideboard stood a bottle of cut-rate whiskey, three-quarters empty, and on the windowsill, behind the couch, they found a dirty tumbler. Joe and Roland asked Martin to sit down, and he proceeded directly to a sort of Barcalounger in brown vinyl. Dad's favorite chair, no doubt, because Martin hesitated before claiming it.

The detectives sat on a comfortable couch with lace doilies on the armrests. Odd, thought Roland, how much apartments in one building could differ. He and Joe had been in apartments exactly like this, in matters of layout, today. The floorspace had been the same, and the locations of the rooms, but what a difference! The younger, affluent tenants had knocked walls down to create vast spaces of their allotted rooms. They had gleaming kitchen equipment, double-glazed windows, discreet lighting— their living spaces were both luxurious and up to the moment. This apartment was merely large and rambling, and he doubted very much if it had changed much in the days since Martin was a baby, sometime after World War II.

"Does anything seem odd to you, out of place?" he asked.

"Dad wasn't much of a housekeeper, was he?" Martin laced his fingers together and then turned his palms out, studying the effect. "If my mother were alive she'd be embarrassed at the mess, but you know how it is, old fellow living on his own after years of marriage."

Fields nodded. In another moment, Martin would reproach himself for not visiting his father more frequently.

"In one way," Martin said, "it's exactly the same as it ever was, if you take away the mess and the dust. Just like it was when I was growing up, if that makes any sense." He stirred fretfully in the Barcalounger, no doubt trying to erase memories of Mr. Crotty reclining in the chair and watching the evening news. *Don't disturb your Dad now*, Mrs. Crotty had probably hissed to the young Martin. *He's relaxing after a long day's work, Martin.*

Something seemed slightly amiss to Fields, who had had cause to explore grief in Irish-American families before. "Have you any brothers and sisters, Martin?" he asked.

"Oh, God," whispered Martin, sloping forward in the unaccustomed recliner. "I had a brother, his name was Mike, but he died in Vietnam in nineteen seventy-two. My mother could only have us two. It was up to me, wasn't it? I should have visited more often."

Riding down in the elevator, on their way to the morgue, Fields thought of his earlier reflections about Barnett Seawright. If the murder of Seawright did prove to be unsolvable, it would be precisely for those reasons that Mr. Crotty's murder—if it was murder—would eventually be revealed. No Martin lurked in Seawright's background, no guilty relative or observer would surface to point the way to a solution.

Mr. Crotty had at least this one living repository of guilt, as well as a host of neighbors who were outraged by his sudden death. Mr. Crotty might have unbearably irritated some of those neighbors, but at least he had made his mark. He would not go unremembered.

Seawright had inspired no real passion, Roland believed. Many had disliked him, but simple dislike was not, usually, a motive for murder. He had passed through life without making the mark Mr. Crotty had achieved.

Nobody had ever loved him, and nobody had ever taken advantage of him in any memorable way, unless you counted the final confrontation in the laundry room.

Mr. Crotty's death was going to cause a much greater stir than Seawright's, and in this one small thing, Roland thought, nature had finally got things right.

THIRTEEN

DO NOT LET ANYONE, REPEAT *ANYONE*, INTO THE BUILDING UN-
LESS YOU ARE SURE OF THEIR IDENTITY. EVEN IF YOU ARE EXPECT-
ING DINNER GUESTS OR A DELIVERY BOY, DOUBLE-CHECK BEFORE
RINGING THEM IN.

Sarah read the notice posted in the little glass box and thought
that the writer had been someone other than Monica, who could
never have contained her message in four brief lines. Perhaps it
had been one of the cops. Now that Mr. Crotty's death was
being treated as a murder, it certainly made sense, but it had
been a rule for years in her building to double-check on callers.
Long ago an old lady had been relieved of her handbag because
Monica Platt had let the thief in, thinking he was from Western
Union. There had been an interminable lobby meeting during
which the rules had been pounded into them. She doubted very
much that any of her neighbors would depress the intercom
button at random. How had Mr. Crotty's assailant gained access
to the building? It troubled her, because there were two possibilities. One was that the intruder had looked so respectable
that he or she had simply waltzed in behind a shareholder and
escaped scrutiny. The other was that the killer lived in the
building, and that seemed impossible. Who could want to kill
both Seawright and Mr. Crotty?

She became aware of a sniffling sound and turned to see
Maryanne, who was perched on the radiator cover, her mail
bunched in her hand, apparently weeping.

"What is it?" she asked, going to sit beside Maryanne. "Bad
news in the mail?"

Maryanne threw her mail on the floor and stomped on it.
"Mail!" she sneered. "You call this mail? 'Congratulations,

Maryanne Francini! You may have won $1,000,000.00!' I'll tell you something, honey, I'm going to need a million if I want to find a new apartment, and so will you."

Sarah was confused. It seemed best to let Maryanne rant for a bit, since she always came back to the point eventually.

"That Adler bitch cornered me in the elevator and said even *I* must see we need a doorman now. I actually believe those Yups are glad poor Tim got killed because the new Board of Directors, if we ever get one, will be sure to vote for a higher maintenance and twenty-four-hour security."

"Not necessarily," said Sarah, feeling the chill of dispossession already. Where would Maryanne go, if forced out? Where would *she* go? "We could run, you and I," she said. "If Monica stayed on, that would make three votes against a doorman. Three against two."

"Who'd vote for me?" Maryanne scrubbed at her eyes. "I'm a counterterrorist, remember?"

"They don't know that, do they?"

"Not yet," said Maryanne grimly, "but the way things are going . . . Last night I woke up at three-thirty because a car alarm was making this terrible noise. Did you hear it?"

Sarah shook her head. She seemed to have an ability to sleep through street noise.

"It wasn't just that ear-splitting, wailing sound most of them have. It had an added dimension, as if they'd hired an avant-garde composer to make it even more loathsome. It went up and down in little burbling riffs." Maryanne shuddered. "It was so vile, so disgusting. Do you know what I did?"

"Egged it?" Sarah smiled, to show that she remembered the time they'd thrown an egg from her window at a drunk who wouldn't stop singing. She'd been giving a dinner party, and everyone agreed that the egg would make a statement. She, Sarah, cheered on by her guests, had thrown it wide of the mark. Nobody had intended for the drunk to be hurt, and he had, in fact, moved on.

"Hardly," said Maryanne. "I save glass bottles now, keep them near the window in my bedroom. Anything will do—Mott's Apple Juice bottles, wine bottles, anything. I grabbed a

Mott's and looked out the window. I didn't want to hit the wrong car, of course, and it's hard to tell sometimes. The streets were absolutely deserted, and the noise could have been coming from any of a dozen cars. What to do?"

She turned and queried Sarah, as if the words "what to do" were part of an actual examination. Her dark and lively eyes were dancing now, as if counterterrorism, with its difficult decisions, had sexy overtones.

"I don't know," said Sarah.

"I put on my coat over my pajamas and got into my snow boots, so I'd look fairly normal if anyone saw me. I was about to let myself out, when I remembered Tim's demon on the fire stairs. 'Is this wise?' I asked myself. It was all so damn frustrating, Sarah, and so *crazy*. I mean, here I was, armed with my apple juice bottle, ready to mess up a car that had woken me up when all I need to do is sleep—"

"Sure, I see," said Sarah soothingly. "What *did* you do?"

"I went back to the bedroom and the siren had stopped. Just like that. I suppose they have a built-in timer. But the point is, I was so wired and angry I just hurled that sucker down on the nearest car. It made a great sound!"

Sarah imagined the satisfying noise the shattering glass had produced, and wondered what would happen to her friend if anyone connected Maryanne to the multiple acts of vandalism which had begun to appear in the neighborhood.

She was sure Maryanne was behind the spray-painted message now gracing Columbus Avenue in Day-Glo orange, the one which said STREET OF GREED. She was also sure that the theft of the lobby's brass ashtray, a fluted affair mounted on a pedestal, was the midnight work of Maryanne Francini.

"I don't think the ashtray was such a good idea," she said tentatively. "I don't want to see you get in trouble."

"Ashtray?" Maryanne frowned. "What ashtray?"

Sarah nodded at the empty place where the expensive ashtray had been until yesterday. Maryanne hunched over, picking her discarded letters from the floor, and mechanically ripping them to shreds. "I didn't take the stupid thing," she said. "For one thing, I don't steal. For another, it's exactly the sort of thing I *don't* want to happen. It gives the doorman people more ammunition."

"Well, you're right, of course, I hadn't thought of it in that light, but who on earth would steal an ashtray? I suppose the brass is valuable, but I can't see anyone from this building needing to fence some hot brass."

They were both quiet then, remembering Mr. Crotty's trips to pawnshops on Monica's behalf. His death saddened them as much as the fact that they had tried to avoid him so often while he lived. "I've got to go," Maryanne said. "Just tell me something before I do. Did that detective, Fields, ask if you'd ever seen Tim's fabled war club?"

"Yes," said Sarah, "I assume he asked everyone. I never did see it, though. I'm not even sure it really existed."

Maryanne paused, as if about to confide something, but just then Jewel came in from outside, pushing Jeremy in his stroller. She was followed by the other West Indian au pair, and their birdsong voices rang in the lobby with such a cheerful and reassuring normalcy that Sarah felt her conversation with Maryanne had been from the Twilight Zone. She waved good-bye to everyone and fled the building.

At Broadway she headed uptown, dodging people in the bottlenecks formed by the scaffolding which seemed to be everywhere. Something to do with Local Law #10, it was said, but more likely a sweetheart contract between the city and a client. She had run out of typing paper and had to go ten blocks to get the kind she preferred. It was cold again, but she could almost sense the presence of the pernicious New York spring beneath the blustery wind. It could arrive as early as February, and, like the earlier warm spell, seemed febrile and ugly to anyone who had lived in a place where there really were four seasons. Spring in Manhattan reminded Sarah of an unwelcome acquaintance with sweaty palms who came and stayed too long.

She had asked Fields why he mentioned the war club, and wished now that she hadn't. Mr. Crotty's skull had apparently been shattered much more effectively than a fall down a short flight of stairs could have done. It was consistent, Fields said, with a blow to the back of the head. The position of the blow was why there was so little blood, as opposed to the blood that would have been shed if he had been struck on the forehead or crown of his skull. The forensics lab had discovered minute traces of paint mixed with Mr. Crotty's brain tissue, suggesting he had been bludgeoned with an object painted red and black. If Mr. Crotty really had possessed a Samoan war club, and if he had, unknown to the other shareholders, carried it on his proposed patrols, it was likely to be the instrument of his murder.

She felt slightly sick, thinking of Mr. Crotty's head, his *tissue*, and walked over to lean against the wall of a bank. Directly in front of her was a bus shelter, and inside it was a man reading the New York *Post*. She could see the large black letters as he turned a page: "Co-op of Death."

Co-op of Death? There was something miraculous in the *Post*'s ability to turn out consistently terrible headlines. She could picture the men who composed the heads snickering with glee over the Co-op of Death. It was all very well for them—they didn't have to live in it.

Phoebe was feeling as bored as she could ever recall in her seven years. Who wanted to be at dumb Adventure Playground when it was so cold, anyway? She would have preferred to have come home with Milagros from school and watched television, but this was not allowed. Her mom didn't permit much TV, only for special children's programs, and Milagros was being nasty, not like she used to be. Phoebe remembered how it had been when Milagros had first come to live with them. She had been so much fun, and Phoebe had agreed with Megan, for once: Milagros was the best! She let them watch cartoons sometimes, if Mom wasn't home, and she often slipped them M&Ms or other candy when they were being especially good and not quarreling. Mom didn't allow candy, either, and once, when she caught Milagros pouring Hershey Syrup into their glasses of milk, she had looked like she was going to explode.

Milagros kept the syrup in her room because she liked to make chocolate Cokes. She had explained that all she took from the Adlers' fridge was the ice. She bought the Cokes and the chocolate at Food World, but Phoebe's mother didn't seem to care about that. She cared only about teeth and bones and good, healthy diets, and poor Milagros had said she was sorry and it would never happen again.

Phoebe began to move around the perimeter of Adventure Playground, unnoticed by Milagros. Megan was playing with Jake and Freddie Spooner, screaming like the stupid baby she was, and Milagros and Teresa were having a conversation. Normally, Phoebe liked to listen in on conversations. She'd been able to pick up quite a few interesting facts in the course of eavesdropping on the au pairs. She knew that Jewel had a boyfriend named Selfridge, and also a little girl of her own. Jewel's mother looked after the little girl, who was about Megan's age. She also knew that someone Teresa liked was in jail back in the place where Teresa came from. But today she didn't seem to want to listen in.

Daringly, Phoebe slipped out the gate of the playground and began to walk around it. She was heading for a tiny stand of trees above Tavern on the Green, where she thought she would observe them from a distance. Milagros was wearing a bright green beret today. As long as she kept her eyes fixed on the green, she would be obeying. She tried to remember how long ago it had been, that time when Milagros had let her play with her blusher. Before Christmas, for sure. Back in the time when there'd been M&Ms and television.

Everything had changed now, and it was all because of some people getting killed in the building. Phoebe wasn't disturbed by death in any way. It happened to old people—look at her grandmother—and you could expect to get killed when you grew old. It was natural. What wasn't natural was the way Milagros had started denying them everything that made life worthwhile.

Phoebe made a sawing motion with the beige scarf tied around her neck. She hated it and wished she could have a green one, like her nanny's beret, or high purple boots, like Teresa. She began to feel very sorry for herself. Megan and Jake and Freddie seemed a million miles away, and no one had noticed that she was hiding in the little forest. For something to do, she scrabbled with her mittened hands at the undergrowth. Once she'd found chestnuts on the ground, and some acorns, but she didn't think there would be anything so nice in the wintertime. A girl at her school, Gracie Square Academy, had told her that all you found in Central Park was Coney Island Whitefish, which was something dirty to do with grown-ups.

The trouble was that grown-ups thought children didn't understand, when they did. Phoebe understood that Milagros was being nasty because otherwise she'd be sent away. If Milagros didn't make Phoebe and Megan eat celery and carrots, if she persisted in letting them have fun, then *Ruth*, her mother, would make Milagros leave. Even as she was thinking this, Milagros let out a little shriek of happiness and tossed her long, black hair beneath the beret. She sent a flashing look in Megan's direction, and then, satisfied, bent back toward Teresa. When would she notice that Phoebe was missing?

Paddling her hands in the dead leaves in agitation, Phoebe encountered something large and round. It was not a tree root, and she didn't think it was a Coney Island Whitefish either. Scraping away, she uncovered a dead pigeon. She had been feeling its rounded breast. The pigeon's eyes were glazed and dirty, like old dimes. Its neck was smeared with something that looked like the iodine Phoebe dreaded. In fact, the pigeon's neck was hanging from its body, as if someone had practically cut it off!

Phoebe knew not to touch dead animals or birds, which were full of fleas. Milagros had told her all about the danger the time her hamster had died. Something called an armadillo was the worst. She felt excitement streaming through her body as she regarded her find. Her eyes snapped open, her heart pounded against her ribs, and a plan began to form. She could hear her own voice asking Milagros about the chickens, and Milagros replied:

"It doesn't *have* to be chickens. You could use a pigeon, or a dove."

Santaría. It was for getting what you wanted. Milagros had told her so, that time in the nanny room. It involved candles and water and statues and dead animals. Phoebe knew how to get all the components, except for the dead animals. Now she had miraculously been given the means to complete the circle. There was no way she could bring the pigeon back today, but tomorrow she would insist on taking her bookbag to the park. With her hands safely protected from fleas by the mittens, she would bring the dead bird home.

Phoebe reburied her find, working industriously, and left him where she had found him, in the crook of a tree's roots, covered with leaves. Then she rejoined the little group in Adventure Playground, cheeks still burning with the audacity of her plan, and discovered that no one had missed her.

At about ten that night Roland Fields, who had been rereading the forensic pathology reports on the two co-op victims, got a call from a woman whose voice sounded slightly familiar. It had rung through on the day-or-night number, and he suspected that he was at last about to get some small bit of information from that embattled building off Columbus Avenue.

She identified herself as Sarah Mason and said that she lived in apartment 7B, and then he knew her—a blond woman, late thirties, polite but a bit opaque. She was a writer, and she had a writer's way of answering questions, choosing her words carefully, occasionally editing herself. He thanked her for calling and asked what he could do for her.

"I have information I think you should know. I haven't told anyone else, except for one neighbor, and we both agreed it didn't matter, once the truth came out." She paused, and he could hear her lighting a cigarette. "I am referring to the death of the bookstore owner, the death that was considered a homicide until the coroner's report said the man had suffered a coronary?"

"I remember, Ms. Mason," said Fields. He felt the disappointment which comes of being led down the wrong road. He had thought his informant was going to come up with some remembered detail about that damned war club. "It wasn't one of my cases, but I surely remember it."

"I know who moved the body into the window," said Ms. Sarah Mason, sounding as apprehensive as she was ever likely to sound. "He actually called me, although he'd never say where he was calling from."

Fields listened patiently while the woman explained her relationship to the bookstore clerk. He realized that she was not used to dealing with the law, still less used to being an accessory to inhibiting the investigation of a crime, so he tried to punctuate her narrative with little homey vocal sounds. He did not interrupt her because he wanted to know why she had called now rather than after the first murder.

"It only just occurred to me tonight—" Again she paused, trying to marshal her thoughts. "I thought that if the man in question had been in hiding all this time, and if Mr. Crotty was killed by some mysterious intruder— It occurred to me the man in question might possibly be hiding in our building. I know it sounds insane, and I honestly don't think Gordon Childs is capable of murder, but it *was* something the police didn't know, and under the circumstances—"

"It was quite right of you to call, and I thank you for doing so, Ms. Mason, but Mr. Childs turned himself in to the Twentieth Precinct after the first true homicide, the one involving Mr. Seawright. He had an airtight alibi, and any charges were dropped in the bookstore affair. Mr. Childs has gone to Florida."

There was a thick silence at the other end, and then Sarah Mason's voice, thin and wounded, inquired: "Well, in that case, Officer, or Detective, or whatever is the right way to refer to you—why did you let me carry on my tale to the bitter end? I said 'the man in question' twice, I was so nervous. And you knew all along!"

Roland laughed, although Sarah Mason would never understand why, and then explained that he had needed to know why she had called at this precise moment, instead of earlier. This seemed to mollify her, and she said she was sorry she'd bothered him at such a late hour. "Anytime at all," he told her. "Anything that strikes you as important is something I will be glad to hear."

After she hung up, he returned to the forensics evidence, but his final laugh at her expense forced him to abandon it for a moment. How could she know how out of character the murders in her building were for him? His usual informants were junkies and street people, finks who parted with a little information to ward off the dry heaves or save themselves from a trip to Riker's Island. They did not worry about their syntax while ratting, or whether or not he might assume a sexual contact between a lady writer and a bookstore clerk.

A case he had recently closed had had, as its principals, the usual cast of characters in a New York City homicide. The victim was a young Puerto Rican mother of two children, the "perp" her common-law husband who had compacted three of her vertebrae and then hurled her from a fire escape. The link to these everyday acts of violence had been a Salvadoran transvestite who had provided Fields with the name of the crack dealer who had been supplying the neighborhood, and who had been palling up to the common-law husband. The crack salesman had nourished grandiose visions of a franchise in certain sections of East Harlem, and it had been the dead girl's misfortune to question the whole endeavor.

It was all very far removed from Sarah Mason's sphere. On Columbus Avenue they thought that life and death was a matter of where you drew the line at ordering out for pizza.

The instrument with which the common-law husband had broken his wife's vertebrae, before killing her, had been a hammer. Fields thought it was all too symptomatic of the co-op case that Mr. Crotty's murderer had been obliged to use an ornamental artifact.

The deaths of the two men had been similar in one way—neither had shown evidence of fighting off the attacker. No bits of flesh or traces of blood had been detected beneath their fingernails. They had both been surprised, at the moment of their deaths, and in some way acquiescent. Seawright in the laundry room, and Crotty on the fire stairs. They had either known their killers, trusted them, or been overtaken with a savage swiftness. To what purpose? Given their very different positions in life, *why?* It didn't make sense.

FOURTEEN

At the big general meeting late in January, the one when elections were supposed to take place, the shareholders all wore uneasy looks. After the first killing, there had been a sort of collective, if suppressed, exhilaration among them, but now they were afraid. No one seemed more afraid than Monica, who appeared sadly diminished. Where always before she had risen to the occasion by wearing something bright and eye-catching, and as much jewelry as possible, she now appeared in a pair of formless brown trousers and an unbecoming sweater. Her face looked drawn to those who knew her best, but the real change was something everyone could note: Monica had very little to say.

They sat in the unflattering light of the lobby, shuffling papers and looking down at their hands, not wanting to make unnecessary eye contact. Even Allen, so cheerful behind his surgical mask at the last meeting, was subdued, and Douglas was notably absent. Everyone was aware that the elevator doors were not going to part and reveal Mr. Crotty, kitchen chair under his arm.

The managing agent, together with the two lone members of the board, Monica and Ed Knowles, sat at the long table borrowed for these occasions, and Ed Knowles seemed about to call the meeting to order when a surprise guest arrived.

There was a little gasp from Fay Spooner, who thought the black detective had come to announce that he'd apprehended the murderer. It would have been so satisfying, so like one of those wonderful, old-fashioned movies where all the suspects are gathered in the library to hear the denouement, that Fay wanted to weep when Detective Fields announced that he felt it would be instructive for him to observe the proceedings.

"Where's his partner?" Mrs. Adler asked her husband.

"He wasn't a *partner,*" Joe told her, speaking with a quite uncalled-for asperity. Lowering his voice to a whisper, he instructed Ruth that detectives in Homicide had dozens of other policemen to aid their investigations, but they were essentially loners. Fields was in charge.

The man in question, wearing what looked like a very expensive cashmere overcoat, walked gracefully to the steps, where the smokers had been isolated, and sat somewhere between Maryanne Francini and Sarah Mason and just below Mr. Spooner, who had quit smoking three years ago and recently taken it up again.

The managing agent called the meeting to order, and then Monica was required, as Secretary, to read the minutes of the last meeting. She did so in a nervous, quavering way, and with none of her old élan. What she read was a dreary litany of jobs contracted to roofers, electricians, and plumbers. When she had finished, the vote to approve the minutes was unanimous.

Ed Knowles, who had been sitting with his arms wrapped around his narrow torso during Monica's recitation, now freed himself, nodded judiciously, and slid forward in his chair.

"I think I am not exaggerating when I state that this corporation is in a peculiar, indeed a *unique,* situation," he said. "Our bylaws clearly mandate a Board of Directors comprised of five shareholders. We have lost our President in a grotesque and unforeseen manner, and earlier one of our members resigned."

"He sure did," Allen said clearly, and in venomous tones.

Ed's eyes skittered in Allen's direction and then retreated. "When Douglas resigned his post, we had every good reason to believe that several shareholders, Joe Adler among them, would be willing to serve. Now Joe has informed me that an exceptionally busy schedule will prevent him from assuming the duties of a fully cognizant member of the Board of Directors. No shareholder has put his or her name forward as a candidate in this election, and after long consultation with our managing agent, Bob Grout, we have decided that the best course we can follow is to seek your mandate for an amendment to the bylaws. You all have copies of the amendment, but let me make it perfectly clear. We are proposing to reduce the Board to a body of three—Monica, myself, and Bob Grout."

Now or never, thought Sarah, preparing to implement the battle plan she and Maryanne had worked out. "Excuse me," she called out. "Are you prepared to take nominations from the floor?"

Ed blinked, and then hurled himself into a consultation with Bob Grout. He emerged looking weary. "I am informed," he said, "that the bylaws do not preclude nominations from the floor."

"I would like to be considered as a candidate," said Sarah.

"We'll need a second on that, Sarah."

"I second the nomination!" shouted Maryanne in a voice rather louder than the shareholders had anticipated.

"Well, you see," said Ed Knowles, smiling like a crocodile, "this puts us in an awkward position. Your addition to the Board, Sarah, would make an even number again."

"Not if you dropped Bob Grout," said Allen. "*He* doesn't live here."

"But the amendment, prepared for you to ratify, specifically calls for Mr. Grout's presence on the Board," said Ed Knowles. "This suggested irregularity would call for more paperwork."

"No it wouldn't," cried Allen. "It's not in the bylaws yet. It hasn't been voted in, so it doesn't exist."

"But there does remain a problem," said Ed Knowles with a false patience calculated to make them all feel like badly educated children. "To ensure a policy of fairness, we must vote in an uneven number of officers or we'll be forever locked into an unbreakable decision, or a whole series of them." He made a hand gesture, as one who wished to be deemed unassailable, a plain purveyor of the truth, and wormed his way back into his seat.

"So, okay," came a voice almost as familiar to the shareholders as Monica's. "Somebody nominate me. God knows I don't need the aggravation, but somebody's got to do it."

"I nominate Ida Strabinski," said Sarah.

"Second!" shouted Maryanne.

Allen applauded and Ed Knowles looked furious. He turned

once more to Grout and said something in tones so low no one could hear him. The agent replied in kind and Knowles gave a kind of shrug of resignation. "I think perhaps we ought to consider the original plan a little further," he said.

"Why?" Mrs. Strabinski looked outraged. "I am ashamed of you, Mr. Knowles. Here we have back our original number, five, and you are still trying to get us to amend the bylaws. Why, I ask you?"

Knowles gave a rather forced smile, acknowledging defeat. "Well, put like that, Ida, I suppose you're right. We'll still have to amend them so that Mr. Grout will be able to serve, but—" He shook his head to indicate that he was too gentlemanly to object to her presence on the Board. The election which followed was a mere formality.

Sarah saw a smile cross the detective's face and wondered what it signified, whether Fields sympathized with Ed Knowles or sided with the small group that refused to have the Board made even smaller and more secretive.

"It was our custom after these elections," said Ed Knowles, "to declare an executive session, usually held in Barn Seawright's penthouse. I don't think that will be necessary tonight. The new members will be notified when the next meeting is called."

"Excuse me," said Sarah, "but the new members, like the old ones, have the right to some input about meeting times. You can't simply *summon* us."

"You're right, of course," said Knowles with exaggerated courtesy. "If you and Mrs. Strabinski would care to submit dates when you can't be available in February, please notify Monica."

At mention of her name, Monica twitched. Sarah thought she really did look unwell, and put it down to the chain of horrible events that had culminated in Mr. Crotty's death. Or at least, she hoped they had culminated then, and that there was no further mayhem in any of their futures.

The meeting broke up quickly then, and Sarah was surprised when Fields asked if he could talk to her and to Maryanne.

"It would have to be in Sarah's apartment," Maryanne said.

"Mine's a real mess at present." Instantly, Sarah knew that her friend had left some of her counter-Yup paraphernalia lying around, and didn't want Fields to see it, but what? Cartons of spray paint? A fresh supply of single-edged razor blades?

"No problem," Fields said. "Aren't you a little fed up with the Co-op of Death?" He grinned now, fully and sweetly, for the first time. "Why don't you both meet me at Raider's, round the corner, in ten minutes?"

Sarah had been in Raider's only once and didn't like it. Maryanne actually hated the place, because she suspected the "raiders" of the title referred to the corporate kind. Nevertheless, they rode up to get their coats, met again in the now empty lobby, and walked around the corner to the overpriced wine bar, which was actually a regular bar and once the site of a Mom and Pop deli.

Fields was sitting at a table near the rear of the long, marbled corridor reserved for diners, away from the bar. He had picked a choice spot, because a real fire burned in a little recessed fireplace not five feet away.

"This place is half deserted," said Sarah, slipping into a chair. "Why is that? Every time I pass it it's mobbed."

"That's because 'L.A. Law' is on tonight, starting in just about"—he consulted a very expensive-looking watch—"thirteen minutes."

"Come on," said Maryanne, "even *I* have a VCR."

"Actually, the word is out. This place is going to close soon, so the clientele has moved on to the next hot spot."

Sarah looked around at the lighting fixtures, so prettily shielded in pink and green porcelain, at the costly green linen napkins set out at each place, at the stippled marble floors, and thought what a waste it all was. Raider's had done very good business, but apparently not good enough to meet the demands of a landlord prepared to triple an already crippling rent.

"Good," said Maryanne. "I hate this place and all the others like it."

"I'm not overly fond of it myself," said Fields, "but it had the advantage of being close to your building, and you've got to admit it's quiet now."

A blond girl with her hair in three colossal bunches came to take their order. Her voice was peppy in a Texas kind of way, but she looked depressed. Sarah ordered a scotch and water, Maryanne a rum and Coke, and Fields said he would have another Double Happiness beer. The waitress snatched away the linen napkins and said "sure thing" in a weary voice.

Maryanne had already begun to root around in her purse, but Fields shook his head and said, "Ladies, please! I'm paying, if you don't mind. I need to pick your brains, and it's a time-honored custom that the picker pays for the pickees' wisdom."

"So that's what I've become," said Maryanne. "A pickee. Why us, for starters?"

"That goes to the heart of the problem, you could say." Fields bent forward, almost seductively, Sarah thought. She and Maryanne had to be on their guard against this clever man who wanted to make them feel important. She was acutely aware of danger in a way she had never been before, and this Homicide detective, wearing shoes she could never afford, had managed to rearrange her ways of thinking about the NYPD.

Because she had never been involved in a crime of any real consequence until now, her associations with city cops had only included brushes with the portables, the uniformed men who pounded the beat, their spreading midsections draped with uncomfortable pounds of detritus, who helped you if you couldn't find your way to a given address, or responded if you complained about the noise from a forty-eight-hour party. She thought Fields was on the right side, but resented his assumption that she and Maryanne could be flattered so easily.

"Right," she said. "Why us? We're not Monica, in case you hadn't noticed."

Fields laughed uproariously. "Oh, Ms. Mason, and you too, Ms. Francini, I noticed that immediately. You've got three different types living in your building, in case *you* hadn't noticed. You've got the money-is-no-object crew, which used to be headed up by the deceased President of the Board of Directors and whose mantle has now fallen on the shoulders of Mr. Knowles. Am I right?"

"Oh, very right," said Sarah. "Exactly right. The doorman group who want to raise the maintenance."

Fields finished his first beer and held up three fingers, striking one down. "Second group," he said. "This includes those old enough to have successful sons or daughters who were able to buy the co-ops for their parents as investments. This group includes Mr. Crotty, Mrs. Platt, and Mrs. Strabinski, among others. Correct me if I'm wrong?"

"In Ida's case it was a rich cousin," said Maryanne, "but you're basically right, on the right track."

"And all the in-betweens," said Fields, "how do they manage? The people who aren't rich enough or old enough?"

"He means us," said Maryanne. "We're the people in limbo, aren't we, Sarah? Neither here nor there, as it were. Nowhere else to go, just hanging in there by our fingertips. Thanks, Mr. Well-paid Detective. Thanks for reminding me."

Fields' hands shot out and imprisoned Maryanne's in a lightning movement. "Listen, you stupid broad," he said. "Don't cut off your nose to spite your face, as my Aunt Clothilde used to say. I need to know how the goddamn third group makes it, and I need to know for specific reasons. It's important to the case, and I won't ignore it, not for your sake or for anyone else's. I'm not used to investigating deaths in fancy co-ops, and I need a little help here."

Maryanne relinquished her wrist in an aristocratic manner. She slinked into her coat and managed to say, "Sarah, I'm leaving. I don't think our meeting with this creep in the cashmere coat has been at all productive. You can talk to him until you're as green as these walls, but I'm *out* of here."

Sarah felt embarrassed after Maryanne had whirled off so dramatically. "Sorry," she said. "My friend is a little—overwrought lately."

Fields shrugged. "She's just determined to be offended by me. Know why?"

"I think," said Sarah, knowing she would regret it, "she considers you sort of, ah, sort of a Yuppie cop." And then she laughed a little, nervously at first, and Fields also began to laugh, with real intensity. Just as they would begin to taper off, one or the other would say "Yuppie cop," and both would go into fresh gales. The melancholy waitress shot them an envious look.

"Look," said Fields, "I live in Queens, okay? Tell her for me. There is no such thing as a Yuppie cop, certainly not in Homicide."

Sarah sighed, brought back to the true reason she was sitting in Raider's with an attractive, apparently heterosexual, man. "Right," she said. "You've got one pickee left, so pick."

"How do you and your friend manage to own co-ops in this neighborhood?"

"Simple. We were both married when the building turned. Our husbands bought them—remember, the insider price was about one seventh what outsiders are paying these days. We both had relatively amicable divorces, and we worked it out that we'd stay on, with the understanding that if we ever sold out we'd split with them fifty-fifty."

"And do your ex-husbands pay the maintenance and mortgage?"

"You must be joking. In a word: no. In my case, we'd already paid the mortgage off, so I have only the maintenance, but it's hard when you're self-employed. I would willingly move to a smaller place, but what's the use? I'd be paying the same, or more, for a third the space. There's nowhere to go. Maryanne's self-employed, too, and that's what makes us feel so bitter at times. Most of our money is going out for what used to be called rent."

"Mrs. Platt must be scared of a rise in the maintenance, too."

"Of course she is, and that's one reason I was always glad to have her on the Board of Directors."

"Now you're on, too," he said with mock solemnity. "Together with Mrs. S, who I don't imagine would have much cause to rejoice in a hike in her monthly nut. Was that planned, that little announcement about running from the floor?"

And Sarah, who allowed Fields to order another drink for her, told him how Douglas had been made to feel like proverbial dirt by Seawright, and how he had urged her to run. All she'd done was tell Maryanne to offer a swift second, because they'd been imagining they only needed a third member. The business of the managing agent serving had been sprung on them at the meeting, and Mrs. Strabinski's gallant hat-tossing had come as a complete surprise. *

"What else did you notice at the meeting tonight? Was there anything else unusual?"

"Monica. I've never seen her so subdued. She actually seemed terrified."

"And what could make the garrulous Monica afraid?"

Sarah looked at her companion with amazement. "Jesus, Fields, how can you ask? She's a little old lady who's been robbed quite recently, not to mention the fact that two of her neighbors have been murdered, one of whom she'd known for years and years."

He continued to look at her, a professor whose prize student has not come up with the right answer, and Sarah squirmed. She knew that her explanation of Monica's odd behavior had been inadequate, but how she was not sure. It sounded right, but Monica's self-esteem was such that it would take more than the death of Mr. Crotty, the most recent calamity, to penetrate it and turn her into the trembling, self-effacing creature she had been tonight.

"She seemed at her worst when she was reading the minutes of the previous meeting," said Sarah, groping toward an elusive truth. "Normally, she glories in it. It's the verbal equivalent of those newsletters she sends out, with little seasonal stickers. It's her big moment, and tonight she wandered through it like a sleepwalker."

"I've read some of those newsletters," said Fields. "It struck me that one of the biggest concerns was selling vacant apartments, shoveling some money into the Capital Fund from the flip taxes. You currently have an apartment up for grabs, one that isn't complicated by crime or anything out of the ordinary. Just an apartment where an old lady lived. Her daughter has had it on the market for some months."

"Tess Abelson," said Sarah. "She actually died at Food World. But what's the point?"

"Isn't it unusual for a place like that to go begging? It's a very desirable property, after all. Wouldn't you expect there'd be some mention of prospective buyers in the minutes?"

Sarah thought. If the minutes had seemed more boring than usual, it was because they detailed only the myriad ways in which the building was falling apart, and suggested the numerous contractors whose coffers would be made richer by cobbling it together. Always before, there had been a few items, the sort to appeal to the interests of a broader sector of the shareholders. Complaints of the sounds of little feet thudding over uncarpeted floors overhead; tactful resolutions of so-and-so's distress at hearing loud, symphonic music at inappropriate hours of the night; niggling rants about the laundry room, the letter boxes, the rain mats spread down in the lobby on stormy days. And there had been, too, the triumphant announcements of an apartment sold for some unimaginable, fanciful amount, giving the corporation enough extra money to plant a tree in the courtyard or install new clothes dryers.

"Do you mean the minutes had been *edited?*" she asked. "Were they leaving something out?"

"Possibly," said Roland Fields.

"That would account for Monica's nervousness. She thinks of herself as a flowing fount of truth. But who could have forced her to read a false version?"

"What do you think of Grout, the managing agent?"

"We've had so many," said Sarah. "I barely know him."

When they emerged from Raider's it was nearly midnight, and Detective Fields escorted her not only to the door but to the elevator, and then, to her amazement, to her floor. He waited while she fitted her key into the lock. She had agreed to be his fink, his middle-class fink to be sure. He had explained about the junkies and derelicts and prostitutes who were his usual conduits of information, and Sarah had quite seen his point. None of them would be of the slightest use in the current investigation.

Alone in her apartment, Sarah thought she would quite enjoy being a fink for a Homicide detective. Since she was not dependent on any drug, or homeless—at least not for the present—her reward would not be of the monetary variety. Her reward would be the temporary closeness and friendship of an interesting man she might never have met if her life had progressed in the orderly way she had imagined in Indianapolis.

She tried, as she brushed her teeth and prepared for bed, to remember her assignment. It had to do with keys, keys which the former tenants of the building might have indiscriminately given out. Several candidates for this indiscretion presented themselves, but she thought she'd sleep on it and emerge with a fresher mind tomorrow.

Just as she was drifting into sleep she heard a chorus of voices rising up from the street, and knew them to be of no consequence.

Her last waking thought was a wish that Maryanne, no doubt angrily wakeful on the fifth floor, could ignore the noise, sleep through until the morning, and waken to the certain knowledge that Fields was, after all, not an enemy but a protector.

FIFTEEN

Phoebe lay in bed, too excited by the presence of the dead bird to sleep. It was lying, even now, directly beneath her bed where she'd hidden it, and tomorrow she would find a way to sneak it under the bed in her parents' room. She would also get some candles from the high cabinets in the kitchen when Milagros was in the bathroom or something.

For now, it was enough that she'd been able to get the pigeon home safely. She relived the whole adventure, relishing her cleverness, stuffing her fist in her mouth when she felt too much like giggling. First, there'd been the matter of her bookbag, which Milagros didn't want her to bring to the park. "What you gonna do with it in the park, Phoebe? You don't want to carry it around." She had anticipated the objection and planned the perfect excuse. She needed the bookbag for a science project at school; she needed it because her teacher, Mrs. Rosenquist, had asked them to bring in stones they found in the park. "All different kinds, all sizes and shapes," she'd announced.

Milagros had looked doubtful, but she knew her employer prized her daughters' education above all things, so she nodded, giving in.

The stones project had given Phoebe the liberty to snoop around outside the walls of Adventure Playground, though always within Milagros' line of vision. All she had to do was wait until Milagros got involved in one of Jewel's stories, as she invariably did, and then Phoebe had gone to the little mound and squatted in the old dead leaves. The pigeon had been easy to find, and her mittened hands encountered him almost at once. Quick as a flash she opened the bookbag and took out the plastic garbage bag she'd sneaked from the kitchen drawer. It was the smaller kind, used for lining bathroom wastepaper baskets, and it proved to be a perfect fit. In went the dead bird, but only after Phoebe had removed her mittens to separate the clinging plastic and widen the mouth of the bag to admit him. She'd remembered to put her mittens on when she slipped him in.

Then she'd reappeared on the outskirts of the playground, whistling ostentatiously as she bent and selected stones for the imaginary science project. It bothered her a bit that none of the stones she found looked even remotely like containing fossils, but Milagros wasn't really interested in them anyway, and when she showed her a big, dull gray stone she was relieved when Milagros merely clucked her tongue and nodded.

All the way home from the park, she'd felt the weight of the dead pigeon bouncing against her back. It was a scrawny old thing and weighed no more than a pair of Megan's sneakers, but she felt thrilled knowing it was there.

Phoebe scrunched up on one elbow and looked across at her sleeping sister. Megan always slept on her stomach, with her behind stuck up in the air beneath the covers. You could only be sure she was asleep if she had assumed that position, and there she was, off in dreamland, the Gladys Goose lamp revealing her pale gold hair where it fell forward over her turned-aside face.

About her sister, Phoebe had divided emotions. She couldn't understand why her mother and father had decided to have Megan when Phoebe was already there. Why had they needed another child? She knew Megan was the prettier and hated her for it, but she enjoyed looking at her sister sometimes, and even felt a little proud that Megan was so good to look at.

On the other hand, Megan was definitely babyish and uninteresting. It was because of Megan that they had to have the Gladys Goose lamp. Megan was afraid of the dark. This weakness inspired an almost choking contempt in Phoebe, who was afraid of nothing. It wasn't as if Megan's stupid fears were something she'd grow out of either, because Phoebe could remember perfectly well how *she'd* been at four. She made a little catalogue of her own superiority: no nightmares, no fear of the dark, no whining for a Cabbage Patch doll, no tears when Mrs. Abelson's smelly old dog had been put to sleep. She was, Phoebe thought, much smarter than her sister. Being smart was better than being pretty, because smart people, like Dad, knew how to get what they wanted, whereas pretty people, like Milagros and Megan, just got bossed around. Her mother, Ruth, was not pretty, but she thought she was probably smart in some way she wasn't old enough to appreciate yet. What it all came down to was this: if Megan had found the dead pigeon with its skinny throat cut through, she would have been blubbering. She would not, like Phoebe, have grasped the *santaría* business and seen that the bird could help her get what she wanted.

Phoebe sniffed the air in the bedroom and could only smell the air-freshener she had sprayed over the pigeon when it had begun to smell. Lucky for her that there were little cans of it everywhere! Smart as she was, she hadn't anticipated that the pigeon would smell differently after an evening in the steam-heated atmosphere of the Adler apartment. That was going to be a problem, but she thought she could handle it with the air-freshener, or, if the bird really started stinking, like Mrs. Abelson's dog, she might be able to sprinkle it with some of her mother's delicious perfume—the kind that came in a frosty bottle with a little bird-shape for a handle.

That made Phoebe want to laugh, the thought of the bird-handle perfume anointing the bird-thing under the bed. Her mittens were also under the bed, and she would have to think of some good excuse for losing them, since they had been knitted by Milagros' auntie. Oh, it was wonderful to lie in her warm bed and invent ways to confuse the grown-ups who controlled her life!

When Phoebe rolled out of bed, she felt much as she had done when she'd first discovered her prize beneath the leaves. Once more her heart beat hard. Her feet had a will of their own when she strode from her room and peered up the hall. All clear. She could hear the sounds of the forbidden television coming mutedly from her mother's bedroom, and she knew her Dad was away for a day on "business." Milagros was far away in the au pair room, and Megan was deep in her babyish sleep.

In the kitchen she dragged a chair to the cabinets and located the candles. Not the birthday candles which came in little packets, purchased at Food World, but the fat, waxy, yellow ones her mother kept in case of what Ruth called a "blackout." She took only two, the number she thought Milagros had been burning on the evening of her return, and positioned the kitchen chair back in its place. It was easy enough to light the candles from the top of the stove, but what then?

Phoebe's mind raced desperately, trying to solve the problem, and an image of jack-o'-lanterns appeared. She took a saucer from the drainboard and dipped the candles, spilling liquid wax as her teacher had done, and planting them in what turned out to be cement.

She was back in her Laura Ashley bedroom in no time at all. While Megan slept on, oblivious, Phoebe improvised the rites of an alien religion, kneeling on the carpet. It was difficult, because of the mittens. She didn't know if the mittens would make her prayer less powerful, and wondered how she'd be able to sneak her principal find beneath her mother's bed on the following day, but she did know that she was engaged in important business.

Sarah made a list of all the people who had left her building when it had been converted with an eviction clause. They amounted to four: a youngish couple who had simply moved to the suburbs without notable bitterness; a woman without relatives whose husband had died and who was not quite old enough to claim the safe clause, and had left with great bitterness; and Petie, a rather likable young writer who said he'd rather die homeless than get tied down to mortgages.

She studied her list and did not find it very satisfactory. It seemed highly unlikely that any of these former neighbors might have issued spare keys. Petie had had a live-in girlfriend he had planned on marrying, but Sarah couldn't imagine friendly Betty? Becky? creeping back to the co-op to commit terrible acts. Monica was the logical person to call. She was, or had been, the repository of all the building's gossip, but calling Monica now was unthinkable. Whenever she encountered her now, she felt she was seeing a ghost.

She dialed Allen and Douglas' number and got a recorded message: "Hi, you're out of luck because we are somewhere do-

ing something incredibly glamorous and self-fulfilling. For details, leave your name and number and we'll report back later."

"Bet you're both on jury duty," Sarah said after the beep.

She was sitting in her workroom, at the desk where she wrote.
It faced out on the street, and if she looked up she was rewarded
only by the grim facade of the last shabby building on the block,
directly opposite. Often she pulled the blinds, but today she
needed bright light for some reason. A hard winter sun spilled
in, highlighting little motes of dust and gilding the heap of reeking cigarette butts in her ashtray. Her plan to cut down, with a
view to actually quitting at some future date, had gone out the
window with the unsettling events which had heralded her return from London.

She lit another cigarette. What the hell. What use to have
healthy lungs if her fate were to be stabbed or bludgeoned to
death? She didn't really believe she was in any true danger,
because the democratic nature of the deaths argued against a
dramatic Robin Hood Killer; a criminal who could kill both
Barnett Seawright and Mr. Crotty surely did not fit the psycho-
logical profile the newspapers had earlier posited. If, earlier, she
had thought of the murderer as someone who wished to make a
statement about haves and have-nots, she now thought he must
be simply a deranged person who had managed, at various
times, to gain access to the building.

If she managed to stay away from dangerous and isolated areas—the basement, the fire stairs—she could avoid becoming a
statistic.

There! She knew it! She should have shut the blinds because
the vision now invading her privacy was one she had always
tried to avoid at any cost. Just across from her, on the seventh
floor, a woman leaned out of her window, having her look at
what the street might offer. Despite the coldness of the day the
woman, as always in Sarah's experience, was naked, and her
breasts made a tired arc toward the sixth floor, pouring over the
windowsill and settling midway between stories. She appeared
to be airing her breasts, in much the same spirit that her more
fortunate neighbors walked their dogs.

Sarah covered her eyes and heard a voice saying: "Like it or no, we are a Target Crime Area." It belonged to Sarah's earliest days in the building, when she had complained to a neighbor about the eternal squalor and sadness on view across the street. The neighbor had been Ida Strabinski, her new comrade on the Board of Directors.

Ida picked up her phone on the second ring, sounding tough and cheerful. She did not say "Hello" but "Yes?" *Yes*, in tones that implied the caller had better not waste her time.

Sarah explained that she was researching, in a general way, the problem of access to the building. She read aloud her list of those who might have provided spare keys, and heard laughter at the other end.

"You forget something, Sarah," said Mrs. Strabinski. "The so grand mahogany doors! They were installed a year after we went co-op. None of the old keys would fit the new doors, because the locks were changed."

So much for her new career as a fink, thought Sarah. Mrs. S would be a much better informer.

"But what you say is interesting," the lively old voice continued. "It opens up a whole new avenue of possibilities."

Sarah couldn't think of a single one and drew her blinds against the naked woman's presence in her workroom. She was plunged into an artificial twilight.

"Do you remember the Easters?" Ida was asking. "Of course you do. They moved away, to Florida, I think, *after* they bought their apartment. After the doors made the appearance."

She tried to remember the Easter family, and gradually a misty picture emerged. Guy Easter and his wife, Jean, had lived somewhere in the middle of the building. Guy, at fifty, had sported long hair and worn political buttons on the lapels of his corduroy jackets. Jean was often seen in caftans, riding down for the mail. They'd had two teenage children, Sol and Luna. Throwbacks, her husband had said, from the sixties. The parents were old hippies, the adolescents hippies in an age where self-proclaimed social awareness no longer seemed important, or interesting.

"I do remember them," she told Ida. "But so vaguely. I wonder why that is?"

A tactful silence filled the space between them, and Sarah was reminded that the year of the Easters' departure, the year in which they had sold their apartment for a large amount, had coincided with the time of her divorce. If she pushed herself she could recall them perfectly. Sol and Luna were never alone in the elevators. They were always accompanied by a coterie of teenaged friends. Black, yellow, reddish, the friends invaded the elevator of her memory with their SAVE THE WHALES buttons and their laid-back, druggy courtesy.

"The children," she said. "They had so many friends."

"Not real friends," said Ida. "Parkies. They were all parkies, and Mr. and Mrs. Easter always fed them or gave them a place to sleep."

"Parkies?" asked Sarah.

"Those children who live in the park," said Ida. "The runaways, the ones who stay away from school and take drugs and then play Frisbee. Parkies, you call them."

"Of course," said Sarah. "The parkies." The very mention of the word provoked a memory of the odor of marijuana, a vision of Luna once clinging to a thin young man who had persisted in trying to open the elevator between floors. She had felt as if she'd been placed in an emergency room at St. Vincent's Hospital, and been very glad when the doors parted and Luna had dragged the boy's body from the confining space of the elevator and toward the apparently unending charity and liberal goodwill of her parents' apartment.

"Do you think one of the parkies could still have a key to our apartment?" she asked.

"Sure," said Ida, chuckling mirthlessly. "Why not? I never thought to connect those crazy Easters, but why not?"

Sarah asked if Ida knew the forwarding address for that odd and time-warped family, but the Easters—Guy, Jean, Sol, and Luna—had moved from Florida and were now dwelling in Central America or the Caribbean, and Mrs. Strabinski had lost their track.

"Americans," she said. "Take no offense, Sarah, but they are funny people."

"No one was weird in Vienna?"

Mrs. Strabinski made a little hissing noise, and Sarah thought she'd offended her, but when her neighbor spoke again it was with excitement. "Listen, listen," she said. "One of them is still around, one of the old parkies. I saw him all the time last fall, and I wondered why he seemed so familiar. He's in his twenties now, Sarah, but I finally figured out where I'd seen him. Here! Here, in the elevator with those Easter kids."

"Do you know his name?"

"Why would I know his name? I can tell you what he looks like, though. He's still got long hair. Long and thin. Brown hair. He's short and stocky, and he wears those sunglasses that are little mirrors. Terrible to see yourself in someone's glasses, isn't it?"

"Is that all you know about him?" Sarah didn't feel she had enough information to constitute a tip for Fields.

"Also I know you won't see him until the weather gets warm," said Mrs. Strabinski. "He's a street musician."

Perfect. "What's his instrument?"

"Violin," said Ida disgustedly. "It shouldn't be allowed."

"Violins, or street musicians?"

"He has no talent," said Ida. "Not a scrap."

Ruth Adler's apocalyptic feelings were mounting. It was nothing she could put her finger on, just an all-pervasive sense of anxiety and doom. There were little things, missing saucers, and the smell, in the girls' room, of something burning, as if Phoebe or Megan had been playing with matches. There was another smell, too, and this one troubled her even more. In her bedroom the odor of air-freshener was almost overpowering, but it was not the brand she used. It was so unpleasant it made her think that there was something physically wrong with her.

She had read somewhere that people who experienced seizures often smelled strange odors before taking a fit. She thought she should make an appointment with her doctor, but if she was about to be told something awful it should be when she was in a better frame of mind.

She was dressing with some care, wanting to look her best when she met her old roommate for a late lunch. She could feel almost cheerful, admiring the way the deep blue of her silk blouse perked up her winter-pale face. She could hear Milagros puttering in the kitchen, probably getting the veggies ready for the girls' snack. At least things had improved in *that* quarter. Her little talk with Milagros had at last convinced the girl that Ruth was not to be taken lightly, and she detected no rebelliousness in the black eyes when Milagros promised never, never to break the chocolate rule again.

Ruth's fingers sorted through the pretty scarves she kept neatly folded in the top drawer of her bureau. She was debating between a scarf and a necklace when she overturned the little cloissoné dish she used for storing her earrings. They went tumbling over the carpet and Ruth got irritably on her knees to retrieve them. And just to spite her, they seemed impossibly far flung, as if she had hurled them on purpose. One was nearly under the bed, but where was its mate? Odd how the terrible smell seemed to be getting stronger. She would have to ask her cleaning woman if she had used some kind of potent carpet cleaner.

She stuck her hand under the dust ruffles and panned about for the missing earring. Ah, here it—no. Her fingertips were encountering something much larger, something that didn't belong under her bed. Perhaps she *was* having some sort of fit? She closed her hand around what felt like a very old—like a, no, forget it. She brought it out all in one determined movement and then sat trying to make some sense of what she was seeing.

When brain and vision cooperated, and she understood that she really *was* looking at a pigeon with a cut throat, she began to retch quietly. The gagging was followed by sobs of rage and fear, and when finally she could not prevent herself from uttering a bleating scream of protest, Milagros came running.

"Get out!" Ruth cried hysterically. "Get out, get out, get *out*. Don't you ever come near me or my children again."

SIXTEEN

January slipped away into a colder, gloomier February. The building's tenants struggled on, feeling neglected by the police. In this they were wrong, but because the detective had caught no killer, apparently had no suspects, hadn't even been able to locate the weapon which had split Mr. Crotty's skull, they had lost faith in him. They met in the lobby or the elevator, murmuring uneasily.

"I know it sounds incredible," Fay Spooner said to Ed Knowles' wife when they met by the letter boxes, "but it had something to do with voodoo."

Kay Knowles rotated her finger next to her temple. "Then is Ruth—?"

"No, no," Fay whispered. "She didn't imagine it. Fred told me they actually found this ritually slaughtered bird under the bed. The little bitch was trying to put a curse on Ruth, it seems."

"Well, if it was under the *marriage* bed," said Kay, shuddering, "it probably meant she was trying to get rid of Ruth and into that bed herself."

"That's ridiculous, Kay. Joe Adler wouldn't sleep with a Honduran peasant girl in his wife's bed."

"Maybe he would and maybe he wouldn't, but the point is the girl *thought* she could replace her mistress. That's my guess. Where's Ruth gone?"

"She took the girls and went to Connecticut to stay with her parents. I don't blame her. How could you stay in a place where something like that had happened?"

"She didn't leave Joe alone with the girl!"

"Of course not. She fired her on the spot, gave Milagros fifteen minutes to get her things together, and that was that. I sometimes think we do these foreign girls a disservice, bringing them to a strange country and expecting them to adjust to our culture, just like that. And to trust them with our most precious possessions, our children!"

This was, of course, a dig, since Kay's au pair, Jewel, was from a far more exotic place than Teresa, the Spooners' Irish girl. Kay deliberately ignored it, though privately she wondered if they practiced voodoo in Trinidad, and wondered if she might be wise to check under her own bed. She said, "I suppose they went to the INS about the girl?"

"Fred contacted the immigration people immediately, of course. Without someone to sponsor her—"

Ernesto entered the lobby, and Fay lowered her voice to a scarcely audible whisper. "Without them," she breathed, "she'll be deported."

Monica, who was browsing listlessly at the branch library on this morning, had also heard of the voodoo scare. In normal times it would have been bracingly horrifying, but now it seemed just another ugly and senseless event in a life she no longer understood. Robbery, voodoo, murder . . . they all somehow paled beside the terrible threat hovering over her now. They had been very nice at first, very much the gentlemen, oh yes, hadn't they just, but the moment she had tried to voice her opposition they'd moved in on her with their threats. Like sharks after a predator, or maybe it was a prey.

They had explained that the lawsuit wouldn't affect the building only, but would also be aimed at her. She, personally, could be liable for hundreds of thousands of dollars, money she didn't have. What would she do then? She would have to sell her apartment, and the money would all go to meet her legal obligations, and where could she possibly *go?* She might, in the harsh reality of these new times, find herself actually *on the street*. Homeless! Couldn't she see that they were only acting for her own protection?

She could hear them even here, in the library. Nobody had ever spoken to her like that, not even Barnett Seawright. Their cruel words had made her see herself in a light so hideous she couldn't bear to think of it, yet it was all she could think of.

Standing in front of the large-print shelves, pretending to

cock her head with interest at the selection offered there, Monica realized that she had been lucky when she had only the robbery to worry about. The kind of fear she'd known then was positively benevolent compared to what she was feeling now.

Knowing why she'd been robbed didn't help either, since there was no one in whom she could confide. Monica grabbed a book at random and walked unsteadily to an unoccupied table. She sat in her chair, opening the book so that she was, to all curious eyes, appearing to read in the Reading Room, and tried to amuse herself with the only mental game powerful enough to distract her.

If she had to become a shopping bag lady, what would she choose to take with her?

Fields had run Sarah's information about the Easter family through the sophisticated SEARCH computer and come up with only one minor charge against *Easter, Soleil*, the son, who had once been caught in the act of purchasing a nickel bag from an undercover man. He thought there had been no serious penchant for crime in the Easter family, who had been very middle class, and—in Sarah's words—sixties people trying to cope with the eighties. The friends of the Easter offspring were a very different matter. They had been the city's rejects, mainly, the kids who lived by their wits or died by the lack of them. They were the ones who generally ended up dead in the Ramble, or on the Deuce, Forty-second Street, or so wired and scrambled from the assortment of illegal substances they had snorted, smoked, injected, or swallowed, that they were barely human now.

He doubted very much that the Easter kids had appreciated how wondrous the free crib on the West Side had seemed to these ratlike, superfluous rejects, and wondered if the dispensers of all that hospitality had ever considered the consequences. He doubted it.

If one of the parkies had miraculously survived the illusion of safety Sol and Luna, prompted by their parents, had provided, then Fields thought he knew who had killed Mr. Timothy Crotty. He was not dealing with a sophisticated, Columbus Avenue–type murderer, but with a wired and crazy kid. A kid who had crept into an old haunt, trudging there by rote, and used the key he'd preserved from the old glory days to let himself into a safe haven when the weather got too evil.

Such a person could be capable of stabbing imperious Seawright in the laundry room. Defending his turf. He might also be capable of dispatching Crotty—a terrifying image brandishing, perhaps, a war club. A war club which had never turned up, despite as thorough a combing of Central Park as could be expected. He had a theory about that. The alleged attacker would have wanted to rid himself of his weapon as soon as possible, but since the time of Mr. Crotty's death had been established as somewhere between 11:00 and 1:00 A.M., he would have had quite a wait. The streets would still be busy enough to make him conspicuous at those hours. Roland thought he had waited on the fire stairs, maybe even sleeping there for several hours—and here he hoped the man had at least gone to a different landing, because the thought of Crotty and his killer sharing the same landing was decidedly creepy. Finally, in the dead-end hours of the night, he would have been free to slip out of the building, run the block to Central Park, and throw the thing into a ravine or lake.

He felt sure that even now it was lying in the muddy waters of the rowboat lake, but since nobody could prove there had even *been* a war club, he could not justify asking for a drag operation. Another possibility was that an early morning jogger had come upon it and taken a fancy to the thing. The jogger might have cleaned it up a bit, unaware that he was sponging off bits of blood and brain tissue, and at this moment it could be sitting on a mantel on Fifth Avenue or Central Park West.

He was not without his own informants among the homeless, and a man who had made a camp down in the old train yards off Riverside Drive had pointed him in the direction of one Concho, a youth who made a small living by redeeming cans and bottles at a nickel apiece. Concho liked to pitch a little camp and chill out up behind the band shell in Central Park. "Somebody told him his name meant a shell," the train yard man had explained, "and he took it as a sign."

The shadows were drawing in when Fields parked his car near the band shell and went on foot up the hill behind it. He thought it would be a good time to find the mystical youth at home. Whether Concho would be receiving was another matter.

Fields was well aware that homeless people were as individual as their more fortunate counterparts. The man who camped out in the train yards, for example, was thoughtful and intelligent, down on his luck, a man who had lost his job and couldn't find another in time to keep from being evicted. He was still civilized, being new at the game, while others who had been at it for some time tended to be so immersed in the awful business of staying alive that they had lost the power of speech. A few were dangerous, but mainly to each other.

From the top of the rise, he could see the last of the day people leaving the park. They were streaming along, headed for the exit at Seventy-second Street, vacating the premises rapidly now that the light was leaving the sky. Concho's little crib consisted of a filthy brown blanket, a large plastic garbage bag used for collecting his bottles, and a stack of newspapers. Fields knew the boy could not be far away, because there were a few bottles and cans in the sack which he would never leave unprotected. He guessed that the boy was not an addict—nobody on drugs would have the patience to scrabble about in garbage cans for such a low return. It was more profitable to hang out in the Port Authority terminal and sell yourself to chicken hawks, and the pay was better.

"Get away from there," said a voice quite close to Fields' ear. A thin, caramel-colored boy had emerged from the shadows and was regarding him with a mixture of anger and fear.

"Yo, Concho," said Roland, "I'm not messing with your stuff. In fact, I've come to offer you some money. I'd like to pay you for some information. Man down in the train yards tells me you keep your eyes open."

"Maybe." He was dressed in a long, shapeless coat and beneath it a hooded sweatshirt. The effect was to make his head seem exceptionally small and sleek, like that of a water vole. He had very high cheekbones and dark, liquid eyes.

"You a cop, or what?"

Fields merely nodded. "Not long ago an old man was killed in a building just off Columbus. He got his skull beat in. I think there's someone living out here who has a key to that building, and I think he uses it when the nights get cold. Does that make you think of anything?"

Concho edged protectively around so that he was nearer to his sack of bottles. He kept his hands shoved down in the pockets of his coat. When Fields mentioned there was twenty beans for him, he hunched his shoulders in discomfort.

"Hey, kid, Concho, don't make anything up and waste my time. If you don't know anything, I'm probably going to make a little contribution here anyway. Just please don't waste my time, man."

"Okay. I don't know nobody who has any key. I don't know nothing about no old dude got hisself iced." Just when Fields thought the boy had exhausted his repertoire, Concho said: "Maybe you didden ax the right question."

They fenced about then, Fields introducing the topic of war clubs, stabbings, street musicians, parkies, to no avail. It smelled of decomposed leaves in Concho's abode, and also of Concho. "Look," said Fields, "suppose you just tell me anything unusual that's happened out here since the beginning of the year."

The pretty, doelike eyes glittered with relief. Here was something he could apparently answer. "Dude use to be here all the time," he said, "and now he's gone. I never saw him no more after"—he thought, shoving the toe of his dirty sneakers into some leaves—"after sometime last week. He broke out."

"You know his name?"

"Naw. Nobody did, man. He was weird, cause he never talked. I never heard one word out of that dude's mouth, but he was always around."

"Can you describe him?"

"He was a homeboy, taller'n me. Older, too, about twenty-five, say. He wore a black cap pulled down real low, summer or winter, all the time. Another thing is you couldn't touch him cause he *hated* being touched. He was never no trouble unless someone touched him."

"Well, I thank you, Concho. Maybe that'll be some help."

Fields peeled a twenty-dollar bill from a modest roll and then, thinking of the kid's pathetic industry and relative lack of criminality, he gave him two twenties.

"Hey, *thanks*, man," said the boy who had chosen to live near the band shell because the meaning of his street name was magically revealed to him one day. "Fresh!"

Roland worked out how many redeemables the kid would have to amass to earn forty dollars as he walked down to his car. It was eight hundred.

Mr. Crotty's son had left a note in the lobby saying that his father's last will and testament had bequeathed a Samoan war club to one Patrick McCann, and did anyone know where it was?

When Sarah told Fields, he didn't seem as pleased as she'd thought he would. Or rather, he looked pleased, but about something else. They were in the gloom of another expensively fitted-out watering hole further up the Avenue from Raider's. It was called Major League. Ignoring the waitress's suggestion that they might like to try Major League's famous pate with their drinks, Fields reached into his pocket and withdrew something. He held it out on his palm for Sarah to see.

"It looks like the key to the front door," she said. "Shall we compare it to mine?"

"No," Fields said smugly. "It *is* the key to the front door. I've already tried it. Bingo."

"It was the possession, notice I don't say 'among the possessions,' it was the sole possession of a young man admitted to Bellevue the day after Crotty was killed. He had it on a string around his neck."

"Who is he?"

"Nobody knows," said Fields. "No identification, and he isn't talking, but that's nothing new." He told Sarah of the kid who'd put him on the trail of what sounded like a walking catatonic.

"That's a contradiction in terms," said Sarah.

"Well, he's catatonic now. I suppose he always *aspired* to catatonia, but he couldn't have stayed alive if he hadn't kept on the move. That's what got him taken in. A portable, a uniformed guy on the beat, found him sitting in that underpass where the zoo used to be. At first he thought he was dead."

"Drugs?" asked Sarah.

"No, not now. A doctor at Bellevue told me he thought the guy had been a heavy user of psychedelic substances at some point, years ago. Fried his brains."

"That's just like the Easters," Sarah said wonderingly. "Their friends were probably all using drugs ten years out of style." She sipped at her drink, not enjoying it. She was thinking of the boy who lived behind the band shell. "How old was this Concho?"

Fields shrugged. "Seventeen, maybe younger."

"He should have been in school," she said indignantly, and then, because her friend was regarding her with unconcealed amazement: "Look, even I know the score about the expendable kids. I know the shelters are murderous and lots of homeless people would rather take their chances on the streets. I do read *New York* magazine, Fields, and occasionally I even write for it. I wasn't saying he should have been in school in the tones of a Midwestern schoolmistress who wants to see the police take truancy more seriously, you know."

"I know, Sarah. I thought you were going to judge me for bribing the kid instead of taking him home and enrolling him in a Big Brother program."

Sarah smiled her truce and tried to keep herself from thinking of Concho's life expectancy. "So," she said at last, "you've found Mr. Crotty's murderer. I take it you're sure?"

"As sure as I can be, but who knows if the boy will ever talk? It's not a very satisfying resolution, is it?"

The waitress was bringing a tray of colorful drinks to a nearby table. Sarah was aware that Yuppies liked slushy beverages whipped up in blenders but couldn't herself imagine wanting to drink anything blue. "Couldn't he, the guy with the key, be a very good candidate for Seawright's murderer too?"

"Tell me why you think so."

"He could have been lurking around in the basement—it *was* a cold day, remember, when Seawright surprised him. You said he couldn't bear to be touched. What if Seawright grabbed him, as Tim must have done? Isn't it possible that the same power, activated by terror, or whatever, made him club Tim and stab Seawright?"

"What about the knife? Where did he get a knife?"

"He might have had a knife and then thrown it away, just as he threw away the war club." Sarah thought there was something missing in this scenario, and she believed it had to do with the man's extreme reaction to the effort of murdering Seawright. But couldn't he have been driven completely around the bend by being forced to defend his home away from home not once, but twice?

"A street person," said Roland instructively, in a way which both fascinated and maddened her, "likes to travel light. If our overage latchkey child had ever owned a knife, you can be sure it would have been on him when he was taken to Bellevue. A knife is easy to conceal, it's small, it's compact, it can mean the difference between staying alive and ending up as fertilizer in the park. But a goddamn *war club?*"

"But this guy wasn't exactly Mr. Rational," Sarah said. "You're talking about him as if he were."

Fields lifted his glass of Double Happiness beer and saluted her. "I think you'd admit that Barnett Seawright was not the sort of man to do his own laundry alongside foreign domestics? What was he doing in the laundry room?"

"Hah!" Sarah felt she was on stronger ground now. "As President of the Board of Directors, Mr. Seawright was frequently poking around in the belly of the beast. He might have been investigating illegal electricity meters or sizing up the potential for bigger storage rooms or looking for possible improvements to the laundry room itself. Anything at all. He had a *thousand* possible reasons for being down there."

"Exactly," said Fields. "Which is why our latchkey dude would have avoided the basement. The only place he felt safe was the fire stairs, where nobody ever went."

Defeated, Sarah changed the subject and asked about the detective's visit to the offices of the managing agent. As she suspected, Bob Grout had been the soul of courtesy, providing all the building's records for Fields' perusal, including the doctored

minutes of the January meeting. Just as he had learned nothing
of substance from the former Board members of Seawright's
earlier co-ops, he had come away from Bob Grout with no special intimation of the dislike Seawright must have reaped in the
East Sixties, the East Seventies, Central Park West, and her own
beleaguered neighborhood.

If the green-eyed impostor had inspired animosity in his fren-
zied ascent from Midwestern lawyer to Manhattan aristocrat,
those who had felt it were now united in a smooth wall of conventional shock at his untimely end. One did not always *like* the
man, said the wall, but one couldn't imagine exterminating him,
as if Barnett Seawright had been no more than an embarrassing
cockroach glimpsed in the kitchen.

Emboldened by her second drink, Sarah spoke. "Detective
work is all about making connections," she said. "You're very
good at doing that, and I'd be the first to admit it, but isn't it
possible that the whole thing is as simple as it seems? Couldn't
Mr. Crotty and Mr. Seawright be dead because they were in the
wrong place at the wrong time? Couldn't it be as simple as
that?"

"Crime can be opportunistic," he said, "like a disease. I see the
crimes in your building in that light. One thing leads to another, you see?"

Sarah shook her head because she didn't see.

"Monica wouldn't have been robbed if Seawright hadn't
ended up in the fridge," said Fields. His voice was low and
rapid, indicating, to Sarah, a lack of belief. "Crotty wouldn't
have died on the fire stairs either, and the girl from Honduras
wouldn't have to hide out on St. Nicholas Avenue or wherever
she's gone to escape."

"You think it's all connected, then?" asked Sarah.

"For sure," said Fields, signaling the waitress for the check.

SEVENTEEN

It seemed definite now, the rumor that Food World was about to close. The cashiers talked of it openly, clucking at the swiftness of the transaction. "One minute," said Ella, a motherly checker everyone liked, "you're here like every other day for the past ten years, and the next minute—poof! You're out."

Maryanne overheard this remark and felt indignant on Ella's behalf, on the behalves of Carlos and Debbi, Lynda and Tenerife and Javier and all the other employees of Food World who were now to be turned out just because some greedy son of a bitch wanted to open an emporium for jogging clothes, or a mammoth restaurant with Third World cuisine and First World prices.

She felt so enraged she dropped the carton of milk she'd been carrying onto the shelf for soups and left the store, battling her way out of the "In" door. If she had stayed she would have heard Ella and the others telling interested customers where they would be working from now on, at various Food Worlds in three boroughs. Actually, Ella would not have nearly so long a commute now, and was rather pleased. She had not objected to the relocation, merely to the lightning-quick manner in which it had been decided upon.

But Maryanne, oblivious to all these finer points, went back to her apartment convinced that the world had grown so cruel that Ella would soon be homeless, like the boy Sarah had told her about who lived behind the band shell. Sarah was very thick with that detective now, and she was close-mouthed about their relationship, but every now and then she parted with a crumb. Just now, for example, Sarah, who hated unseasonal weather, was aching for a warm spell to flush out some street musician who had once been friendly with those ghastly Easter kids.

Maryanne decided to walk off her anger and headed for Amsterdam Avenue, the least gentrified of the streets in the neighborhood. Even Amsterdam was showing signs of Columbus Avenue syndrome now, but at least it was not yet really *fashionable.* She stopped at a pizza place on Seventy-ninth and bought a slice of Sicilian and a Diet Coke. There were a few plastic-topped tables in the back and some tatty posters of Italian scenes, together with some truly appalling murals executed mainly in tones of turquoise and olive green. No signs of gentrification yet, but she knew when she reemerged on the street she would pass little pockets of anxiety-provoking *niceness.* Cute kitchens serving whole-grain breads and weirdly wholesome soups would give way to breathlessly trendy restaurants, which would in turn give way to the outposts of consumerism that were all that was left of Columbus.

Not, Maryanne thought, tipping her paper plate and aluminum can into the refuse bin, that she hadn't appreciated Columbus Avenue's earliest attempts at bettering itself. It had been little more than a slum when she and her husband had first moved in, and the sight of a few jolly cafés and exotic coffee-bean boutiques had been a welcome one.

The trouble was that nobody knew when to stop. Nobody had the slightest glimmer of a clue. It was either a slum, and Ida's famous Target Crime Area, or it was a place frequented by people who did not shudder, as Maryanne did, at the sight of T-shirts imprinted with the legend SHOP TIL YOU DROP.

Back on the street, she noticed that an old and well-loved bakery was now carrying the familiar sign in its window: *"Lost Our Lease."* And the riot gates over the old *botanica* had a suspiciously final look to them. At the *botanica* they had sold roots and powders as well as statues of Jesus, wearing his crown of thorns. Maryanne remembered going in, years ago, to buy some incense labeled "power" for a friend who feared she would not be getting a promotion at her university.

It had been a kind of joke, of course, but the thought of the power incense led to thoughts of Milagros, who had apparently resented Ruth Adler enough to slaughter a pigeon and place it under her employer's bed. She wouldn't have believed it of the girl, who had always seemed so *modern* in her outlook.

Maryanne walked all the way to Ninetieth Street and then turned back. Her mind was buzzing with images of Milagros, Ella, the boy in the park, and her own inability to survive in Manhattan as a photographer's rep. It seemed she had jarringly fallen, slipped, into the social slot of the very people she'd been worrying about. Perhaps they would *all* end up living behind the band shell. She would have a distinct disadvantage, then, because unlike the others, she had not been prepared to live the life of an outcast.

Passing Verdi Square, a rabbly, triangular space with a statue of the composer much whitened by pigeons, she saw the men preparing to bed down for the night on the slatted benches. The Big Apple clock on top of the bank told her it was 11:47, and 32 degrees above zero. Maryanne was tired from her brisk walk. She plotted the next few hours very carefully. She would go home and set her alarm clock for 3 A.M. She would then proceed to take a very hot, fragrant bath, drink an enormous glass of Bardolino, and sleep until the peeping sound of the alarm summoned her to her last, and greatest, act of counterterrorism.

Teresa, too, had been out walking on that chilly evening. The Spooners were having a dinner party, and Jake and Freddie had gone to bed hours ago, and she couldn't see just sitting around listening to the shrieks of Mrs. S's lady friends wafting in from the dining room. Sometimes she felt safer on the streets than in the apartment, what with all the carrying on. And now, with Milagros gone, the Nanny Gang of Four wasn't nearly as nice as it had once been. Jewel had never really liked her, and Norrie was pleasant enough, but they'd needed Milagros', well, *flair* you could call it, to smooth things along.

She stopped to admire a black dress in a window. It had interesting slashes in the hem, and hung unevenly so it was a mini in some places, practically. Sure, it probably cost the earth and then some. Milagros would have admired it, too. Her thoughts kept returning to the Honduran girl, because she knew she would never have done what they accused her of doing. Even if she hadn't *known*, she would have bet her life on it, but now she did, in fact, know.

Milagros had come that very day to Adventure Playground, strolling up to them as if nothing had happened, grinning at their surprise. She explained she had come to say good-bye, and to clear her good name. "They deportin' you so *soon?*" Norrie had asked, but Milagros had laughed and said she was going to lie low up on St. Nicholas Avenue, where there were plenty of illegals. So long as she didn't hang around her former employers' turf, deportation was the least of her problems. She had met this guy who thought he could get her a job as a part-time barmaid in Spanish Harlem. She spoke rapidly and made it all seem like a great adventure, but Teresa could tell that Milagros still felt wounded at the manner of her expulsion.

"Look," she had told them, perching on a bench and nervously pulling at the fingers of her gloves, "I didn't put no pigeon under the bed, I swear to all the saints. I don't go in for that *santaría.* Well, once, maybe, in a half-ass way, and that's how Phoebe got the idea. It was Phoebe, it's got to be Phoebe, there's no other answer."

They'd listened to the story with fascination and no small amount of horror. "Mrs. Adler has to be told." That had been Teresa's opinion, but Norrie and Jewel had been for not rocking the boat. No good could come of it. Mrs. Adler would never believe it, and even if she did, Milagros would never want to work for her again.

Teresa scuffed her boots as she walked past the glittering windows, acknowledging that she was now charged with two duties. The first would be easy. It only involved making sure that Megan was slipped the odd sweet now and then, say once a week. The other was much more onerous, and no one was telling her to do it but herself. At some point, when Mrs. Adler returned, she was going to have to gather her courage and tell the woman the truth. And if she wasn't believed, she would have to tell Phoebe that she knew, for the child's own sake. Teresa could see her green card flying away on little wings, and all because she understood the concept of guilt so well.

She thought she heard someone call her name and peered about in confusion. The friends she had managed to make on her days off all lived in Queens or the Bronx, and she very much doubted that she was the Teresa being hailed, since nobody from the building would be calling after her so urgently at this elevenish hour of the night.

A blue car had come nosing up behind her, as if in leisurely pursuit, and for a moment she felt afraid. It was dark blue, like the Cortinas the Special Branch at home liked to drive. Then she recognized the face of the man who was beckoning her to the curb, and fear settled at a different level. He was not a white-slaver or the Robin Hood Murderer, so that part of it was all right, but he *was* the detective who had interviewed her after the two murders. Mother of God, what did he want with her?

She walked to the curb and said good evening, burying her woolen gloves with the cutoff fingertips deep in the pockets of her jacket. He might not know it was a fashion and think it branded her as some kind of criminal.

"Why don't you get in the car?" he said. "We'll go for a drive, and then I'll take you back to your doorstep. Mrs. Spooner told me you'd gone out, and I've been looking for you. Okay?" He smiled.

Back home, this was how you got killed, especially in the North, particularly if you were a Catholic. You accepted a ride from someone with a smiling face, and the next day your body was reported in some alleyway or on a wasteground, and the papers spoke of Protestant paramilitary gangs and wrung their hands over the "sectarian war." How was it possible to have a one-sided sectarian war?

"Teresa," said the detective, "I need your help, and I'll be brief. You don't have to get in the car, but it would make things a whole lot easier. I'm parked in front of a bus stop, in case you hadn't noticed."

This made her laugh. A peeler afraid of a parking violation. "If you want to know did I make a copy of my key and give it to someone, the answer is no. You're after askin' us already, and we all said no."

"And I believed you," said the detective. He had a nice way with him, but she knew there was a gun beneath his overcoat. She'd seen it when he'd interviewed her in the Spooner dining room and leaned forward to jot something down.

He sighed and tried once more. "What I want to know," he said with infinite patience, "is some further information about the man who shared your brother's name. Remember? The man who was copying out the names from the intercom box."

"Terry?" breathed Teresa. She remembered the sociologist tenderly, and couldn't imagine what his innocent presence had to do with the investigation of the two deaths. "Sure, Terence doesn't have anything to do with murder, does he?"

"Indirectly he might. Terence hasn't done anything wrong, at least to my knowledge. But he might help me to understand a missing link in my investigation."

Teresa got in the car then, and when Fields asked her if she favored any direction for a drive, she answered, "The Village. Greenwich Village."

As it turned out, she quite enjoyed the drive. He cut through Central Park and angled his way down Seventh Avenue while she repeated the details of her fleeting contact with the charming sociologist. She got a very good view of the Empire State Building, which on this night was lit in red, white, and blue like a very expensive ice cream bar partly shrouded in mist and fog. She was able to observe scores of prostitutes tottering about in high-heeled shoes on their fragile legs, and by the time they were darting about the narrow and confusing streets of Greenwich Village she had answered every question about the mysterious Terence. She had told Fields that she had never heard him mention his surname, described the kind of tablet he had used in his research, reconstructed the dialogue between them, and even offered the opinion that Terence was probably married, since she'd noticed a gold band on his left hand.

On MacDougal Street she declined his offer of a souvlaki or similar refreshment and tried to introduce the topic of Milagros and her innocence in the affair of the pigeon, but he didn't seem too interested. He listened to everything she had to say, and nodded courteously, but his concentration remained on the man who shared her brother's name.

Fields was headed uptown now on Sixth. They were passing the Jefferson Market library, with its tower and Gothic clock face. Across from the library there had once been a prison, a

women's prison, and Teresa hoped she wasn't being ever so subtly intimidated. "I've told you everything I know about him,"
she said. "I only met him the one time."

"Just one last thing," said Fields. "This Terence—what was
his race?"

"Race?"

"What color was he?"

"Ah," said Teresa, "like you. Maybe a wee bit darker."

Fields seemed very pleased with her answer. He grinned and
beat out a little tattoo on the steering wheel. All the way back
uptown they talked of inconsequential things, so Teresa assumed her interrogation was over. Cops, she thought. They
were all a bit peculiar, no matter what country you found yourself in.

As he had promised, he delivered her to the building's door.
"Don't worry," he said. "There'll be no more prowlers on the
fire stairs. You're safe."

Sarah was wakened by the telephone's ring at an hour she
immediately knew was inappropriate. The green printout of the
bedside digital confirmed it. No one called her at 4:04 A.M. She
cleared her throat harshly and then answered, wondering if it
could be Fields. If he was calling at this hour, it had to be something momentous.

"Mrs. Sarah Mason?" The voice was apologetic and official
sounding, both. "Sorry to wake you up at this hour, ma'am, but
there's a slight problem."

"Who's speaking?"

"This is Officer Grady at the Twentieth Precinct. We're holding a friend of yours, I believe. A Mrs. Maryanne Francini?"

Sarah repressed a groan. Maryanne had finally been caught
doing God knew what and now *she* was going to have to bail her
out.

"I think it would be best if you could come over to the Precinct House," said Officer Grady, sounding embarrassed.

"How much is her bail?" asked Sarah, trying to think clearly.
"I don't have much cash in the house."

"It's not a matter of bail, ma'am. It's a matter of releasing her to, um, someone who'll be responsible for getting her home safely. I'd send a car for you, Mrs. Mason, but we're short-handed tonight."

"I'll be there in twenty minutes," said Sarah. Terrific. Here she was at four in the morning, preparing to cab on over to the local precinct and baby-sit Maryanne Francini. And what did it mean, this matter of responsibility for Maryanne? Had her friend gone totally mad, and would she have to be accountable for her if further acts of Yuppie counterterrorism occurred?

The cabdriver who took her to Eighty-second Street was listening to tapes of Moslem prayers with rapt concentration, and she rode the distance with the cries to Allah filling the taxi with a terrible foreboding.

The Precinct House was quiet, and Officer Grady, when he came out to greet her, looked to be about twelve years old. "The truth is," he said, "I've never had a case like this and I don't quite know what to do. I only brought her in because she seemed, ah, kind of hysterical and, well, she's calmed down now and I don't want to have to hold her. Most perpetrators in her line are considerably younger than Mrs. Francini, and—"

"What is it Mrs. Francini was doing when you caught her?"

Officer Grady rubbed his hairless chin as if trying to tame a threatened smile. "She was spray-painting," he said, "on the windows at the Food World on your corner. I haven't formally charged her with anything, if you see what I mean."

Maryanne was sitting alone in a room on the second floor, looking horribly humiliated. She was wearing dark jeans and sneakers and a dark jacket. She even had a dark wool cap Sarah had never seen before. Her urban guerrilla costume, no doubt. "Hi," she whispered, not meeting Sarah's eyes. "Sorry about this."

Sarah explained that the young cop wanted nothing more than to get her out of the Precinct House and pretend the whole incident had never happened. Food World was closing soon anyway, and her vandalism, while reprehensible in Grady's view, would soon be covered up by riot gates.

"The only catch is that I've got to promise him you'll behave.

No more night raids. He's made me feel like I'm your parole officer."

"I guess I wasn't cut out for it," said Maryanne. "I wasn't a very good counterterrorist."

"Look at it this way," said Sarah, stroking her friend's shoulder, wishing Maryanne would laugh. "You've done your bit in the war against Yuppies, and now it's time to retire. You were a good soldier, but your tour of duty is up."

"I was going to give it up after tonight, anyway. I knew it wasn't doing any good, either in practical terms or for my state of mind." She sniffled a little and Sarah was relieved to realize that the smudges of black on her face were merely traces of mascara. For one wild moment she had imagined Maryanne blackening her face like a marine on patrol in the jungle.

"What did you spray-paint on Food World, just for the record?"

"You'll see it," said Maryanne, brightening a bit. "Just the usual. I can't help wishing I'd succeeded this last time. I was going to do three whole blocks, graffiti *everything* up past Seventy-second. Think of it, Sarah!"

Grady seemed very glad to see them go, especially after Sarah guaranteed Maryanne's future good behavior. "Take it easy, ladies," he said.

In the cab Maryanne collapsed with her head in her hands. "You understand, don't you?" she asked. "He wouldn't let me go unless I got someone to pick me up. Who could I call? You were the only one who knew about my—you were the only one who *knew*. Anyone else would have been so shocked and horrified. They might even have thought I was *crazy*."

They got out on the corner and walked across to examine Maryanne's handiwork. Across the windows of Food World she had sprayed in huge letters HEARTLESS, GREEDY, TACKY, PIGS! Beneath it bloomed the single word KILL.

"Kill?" asked Sarah.

"Well, that's what was worrying Officer Grady. I explained that I hadn't had a chance to finish. It took me forever to make him understand."

It had been Maryanne's intention to spray the words which

had once been a famous comedian's line on a popular television show. If she had been allowed to complete her work, all the luxe shops in their neighborhood would have borne signs reading KILL DE LANDLAWD!

EIGHTEEN

It took Fields the better part of the next day to determine that nobody with the first name Terence taught sociology at Fordham, Columbia, or John Jay. There was a Dr. T. L. Vanoakes listed in the Columbia brochure, but when he called and asked to speak to Terry Vanoakes in the sociology department, he was informed that there was certainly a Dr. Thomas Vanoakes in the department, but he was on sabbatical in any case. Music and Art High School had a Terence on the faculty, but this one taught fine art. He very much doubted that the Martin Luther King High School had a department of sociology, but he was about to check anyway when the futility of this scheme hit him with full force.

If what he suspected were true, he ought to be hitting the real estate agencies rather than the schools.

The woman in the first agency was a haughty piece of work, especially when she discovered that he was not a potential client. She was dressed in something that looked like a pup tent, and he was reminded of Barnett Seawright's voluminous trousers.

"That information is strictly confidential," the woman said. Her blue eyes beamed righteousness as she uttered the magic word. She liked it so much she decided to use it again. "We observe confidentiality where our clients are concerned, because that's the way they want it."

Instead of muttering about warrants, Fields shifted tactics. "I am investigating the murder of Barnett Seawright, who was killed earlier this year. Perhaps you remember. He may even have done business with you at some point. I understand he bought a number of co-ops, an unusual number. He was in the habit of moving frequently."

"Oh," said the woman, "that was a *shocking* thing. We all felt so sorry here at Winston, because we were the ones who helped him find the penthouse." She gnawed at her lower lip and came to a decision. "Sure," she said, "I'll let you see our lists for December."

Soon she was clicking at her computer and calling up the necessary names. The name of Barnett Seawright invoked the respect his gold shield had failed to inspire.

There were quite a few names to sift through, and the green letters on the screen were annoyingly deceptive to his eyes. One name looked at first glance to be Terence, but proved to be Laurence. No joy there.

It was the same at the second and third offices he tried, but at the fourth he got lucky. It was an extremely down-to-earth place compared with the others. If at Winston & Co. he'd received the impression that any potential buyer shopping beneath the five-hundred-thousand-dollar mark would be jeered, at Moffatt Properties he felt almost at home.

"I don't know," said the secretary, a small, tousled woman. "Have you got a whatsis? A subpoena?"

"A warrant is what you mean," he replied, falling into the well-worn lines. "No, I don't have one, but I can get one and be back tomorrow. Wouldn't it be easier to get it done now?"

"Yeah, put like that, I see the point. I just didn't want to get in trouble." Moffatt Properties didn't even seem to have a computer, because when she returned she was carrying a file. "Make free," she said. "What harm can it do? You only want to see the names, right?"

He nodded, flipping through the names of those who had been shown apartments in December, and there, to be sure, were the names of Mr. and Mrs. Terence Burgess, who currently lived at an address on West End Avenue and who, by the end of December, had not yet found an apartment. He asked the secretary if she would verify the address of the Burgesses, since there was always a chance, however slim, that they'd found the co-op of their dreams in the weeks that followed. As he had expected, they were still on West End Avenue. He didn't bother to press his luck and ask for their file, both because he was sure

they'd been shown the empty apartment in the target building
and because he wanted to hear the story from Terence Burgess
himself.

He thanked his benefactress, who was obviously having trouble with her contact lenses. "Terry and his wife are real nice
people," she said, mopping gingerly beneath her left eye.
"They're not in any trouble, I hope?"

"None that I know of," he said.

When he stepped out onto the street he noticed that it was
surprisingly mild for a late afternoon in February. Maybe another freak heat wave was about to descend on them. Things got
livelier during warm weather, even so early in the year. His
Haitian-born mother, dead for ten years now, had welcomed
any break in a New York winter, and it seemed ironic that if she
had lived another decade she might have experienced quite a
few cozy, ozone-deprived Februarys. His father, an Alabama
man who had headed north to make his fortune, had departed
Roland's life back in the days when there were still big blizzards
in the Big Apple.

Well, it would make life a little easier for Concho and all the
others living tucked into the city's pockets. Terence Burgess
may not have found the apartment of his dreams, but at least he
could afford to live on West End Avenue. Rejection was so much
more wounding when you'd climbed so far.

Forewarned by the telephone call, Burgess had obviously fab-
ricated some story for his wife, and she was all smiles when she
answered the door at seven-thirty that evening. She was a white
woman, which momentarily surprised him, but the little boy
crowding up close to her was reassuring. He was the color of
very light coffee, and his fair hair was kinky and copious. Mrs.
Burgess had pale brown hair and hazel eyes, and an oval face,
and she wore a patterned tunic over a belly which was, as they
said, great with child. She showed him into the living room and
then melted away efficiently, taking the child with her to some
bedroom where their voices could be heard faintly.

Terence was sitting in a chair near the windows, which were
heavily curtained—proof that the Burgess apartment did not

have, as one of its selling points, a view. He rose warily and held out his hand, and Fields was surprised to see the look of naked terror in his eyes. It was a look Burgess thought he had well under control, but he was mistaken.

"So, then," said Burgess awkwardly, "how is it you think I can help you in a homicide case? I never saw the man in question, you know. We never met. I'm an architect, Mr. Fields. I don't go to work packing a switchblade or a razor. I don't carve up Presidents of some Board of Directors in the laundry room, but I do read the papers."

"I'm not for a minute thinking you had anything to do with the business in the laundry room," said Fields. "Relax, Mr. Burgess."

"Fine for you to say," said Burgess.

He was a handsome man, but he had not yet grown into his looks. In another twenty years, Fields decided, he would be one of those distinguished-looking men who could pass for a Justice of the Supreme Court. The dark hair, so carefully barbered, would by then have grown into a pure white mass of leonine rectitude, a symbol of the man's innate superiority.

"What I'd really like to explore," said Fields, "is the day you represented yourself as a crusading sociologist to a little au pair from Ireland who quite innocently observed you jotting down names from the intercom. The intercom on the building where a man had been quite intentionally deprived of his life."

Burgess held up his hand in a vertical position, as if he were directing traffic, or as if he intended to ward off evil. "I didn't want to alarm her," he said. "She seemed like a nice kid. Do you have a cigarette? I gave it up, but I'd appreciate one now."

Fields extracted the pack of Kools he always carried and offered a light. He, too, had given the habit up, and he felt an actual bodily empathy with Terence Burgess as the former nicotine addict sucked the mentholated poison in.

"Hey," said the architect, expelling smoke. "You ought to take it all in at a glance." His hand made a rotating motion. "Wife pregnant. One-bedroom apartment. Another kid on the way. Rising black architect with white wife seeks suitable accommodation in New York City. Combined assets of married couple sufficient to acquire modest dream. Couple shown apartment of ideal proportions and make enthusiastic offer."

His description of the urban housing odyssey came to an abrupt end. As if ashamed of his hand's collaboration in his story, Terence Burgess lowered the offending part of his body and buried it between his knees.

"And then," he continued, "the couple are informed that their offer has been rejected. They don't have sufficient funds. They are not, finally, respectable enough to live in an apartment just off of Columbus Avenue. They don't earn enough money to give their children the luxury of a separate *bedroom.*"

"Were you told that the reasons for rejecting you were financial?"

"I wasn't told a goddamn thing except that the Board had considered my application and found it unsuitable. They don't have to give any reason, you know. In fact, I found out they're advised *not* to, under any circumstances."

"Why would that be?"

"Oh, I think you know." When Fields said nothing Burgess said, drawing the words out and pronouncing them very distinctly: "Discrimination. Lawsuit. Federal offense to deny applicants for racial reasons."

"And was there anything on your application to make them suspect that you were black?"

"Suspect? I didn't know it was a crime, Detective." And then, "Sorry, I know what you meant. One of my character references was from Councilman Thurston, but I doubt if the members of that board even know the names of Harlem politicians."

Fields believed it was quite possible the Board *had* rejected the architect purely on financial grounds without even examining his other references. "And so you decided to sue them," he said. "You decided to mount a discrimination suit against the corporation and the Board."

Burgess nodded, taking a last furious drag on the Kool, and then, having put away all the ashtrays, he resorted to extinguishing it in the soil of a potted plant. He'd been so furious at the manner of the rejection—so cool and cavalier—he had phoned his lawyer and instructed him to call the President of the Board of Directors and tell him, in the same cutting style, to prepare himself for a suit in Federal Court. Before anything could actually be done, the man was dead, and Burgess had discovered just how much a lawsuit would cost. Too much if what he and his wife could win was the right to live in a building that didn't want them. A large cash settlement barely entered his mind.

"Yes, I see," said Fields. "But when the Irish girl met you at the intercom, Seawright was already dead. If you'd abandoned the idea of a suit, why were you playing sociologist?"

"I only said that so as not to alarm the girl. She was so friendly, and I had to give some reason for writing down her neighbors' names. Now, if I have to give you a reason, here it is, the real one. I was still smarting over being turned down. It got to the point where it was all I could think of. I had it in mind to go there and—I know it sounds crazy—just see what kind of people went in and out, search out some ethnic names on the directory. Anything to determine whether they didn't want me because—because of—"

"Yeah," said Fields. "I got it."

"You won't need a statement, will you? I mean, it can't make any difference now."

Fields did not wish to contribute to Terence Burgess' discomfort by telling him the truth. As he had told Sarah Mason, the crimes in her building had been opportunistic. Because the three members of the Board had been reeling under the threat of a huge lawsuit, Ed Knowles must have seen Barnett Seawright's death as a godsend. Together with the managing agent, he had destroyed the information packets on Burgess and doctored the minutes. There would be nothing to prove that the Board had turned the Burgesses down except for the phone call, which Grout could claim had been a misunderstanding. Because he could not depend on Monica to keep silent, he had robbed her himself, or paid someone to do it for him. And someone had taken the little trumped-up burglary as a sign to renew his efforts at keeping the building safe and been killed for his trouble.

"No," he said to Terence Burgess. "I won't need a statement."

All signs should point to Ed Knowles as Seawright's killer,

but when you examined the facts it seemed unlikely. Seawright would have been just as capable of sabotaging a lawsuit as Knowles—they were allies. Seawright's death, he thought, was a case of someone else taking an opportunity, but what it had been, and who the someone was, remained unknown.

NINETEEN

"Hi," said Sarah. "I know you, don't I?"

She'd discovered him five blocks uptown from her corner, playing his violin in front of an ice cream parlor. Although he was not wearing the mirrored glasses Ida had so disliked, she felt sure it was the former member of the Easter retinue. The longish, thinning hair was right, but above all it was the poor quality of his playing that convinced her.

He looked at her with a little half-smile and then down at the cardboard box containing contributions from passersby. There were only a few coins, and even they were mainly dimes.

"You used to have friends in my building—the Easters."

His smile broadened, became genuine. "Sol and Luna," he said. "Wow. I don't think I remember you, though."

Sarah took the dollar she'd been clutching and dropped it in his box. "I really like your playing," she said.

"Thanks. I just do it to pick up some spare cash when the weather is warm. Isn't it fantastic today for February?"

"Fabulous," said Sarah. By the look of it, he didn't pick up much spare cash. Well, what did he expect? Most of the musicians who played stringed instruments on the streets were really very good. She had loitered nearby, a claque of one, while he'd sawed his way through "I Left My Heart in San Francisco."

"I have a mail room job," he volunteered, "but it really sucks. Only good thing about it is I can vanish for an hour or so and nobody misses me. Like today." He picked up his violin again and Sarah frantically grabbed at his arm.

"I wanted to ask you," she said. "I wondered if you ever hear from Sol and Luna?"

He shook his head. "Not for years. They went to Music and

Art, too, back when it was way uptown. That's where we met, originally."

"There was quite a little band of you who used to hang out at the Easters'."

"They were cool," he said. "Sol and Luna had the best deal, with parents like that. They just, like, opened up their home to anybody, because they were full of love."

"One of them's in trouble now," she said, realizing she was going at this all wrong but unable to stop. She couldn't bear the thought of having to listen to him play again. "Big trouble, poor kid."

Blue, watery eyes narrowed with interest. "Who?" he asked in tones which were distinctly unfriendly.

"I don't know his name. He's a black kid who lived in the park, apparently. He still had his key to the building, and the police think he killed an old man named Crotty. He's in Bellevue now, but nobody knows his name because he won't speak." The information tumbled out. There was an unreal quality in trying to coax information from a kid with a violin in his hand, while all around them people emerged from the store licking hand-dipped ice cream. And the kid seemed very tense, too, as if he were trying to make a calculation.

"Apparently this boy always wore a black wool cap, summer and winter."

Recognition flickered in the blue eyes, but he was still struggling with something. "His name's Tyrone," he said in a tight voice. "Tyrone Warren. No, Williams. That's it, Tyrone Williams. He was always weird." He lowered his violin and held it at his side, swinging it back and forth. "I guess living out in the park made him even weirder. That's why he had a key to the Easters' place. None of the rest of us had keys, only Tyrone. That's because we had homes of our own, but Tyrone just lived with his grandmother. Sometimes he stayed away from her apartment for days at a time, and the Easters worried about him."

"Yes, well, it's all a great shame," babbled Sarah. "You take care of yourself, now."

"Wait, though. If you're in contact with the police, I think you ought to tell them about Tyrone. He probably killed that other guy, too. The one that was in all the papers. He always used to carry a knife, everywhere he went. Like I carry my violin. Tell the police. Do you want me to write down his name, so you won't forget?"

"I'll remember," said Sarah. For some reason the sight of so many tongues licking so many mounds of pricey ice cream was beginning to sicken her.

"I must run," she said. "Good-bye, ah, I don't know your name."

"Everybody just calls me Lucky," he said.

Fields took great pleasure in flashing his shield at the reception desk of the midtown office where Ed Knowles worked. The man was getting off very lightly, so at least he could see that Ed Knowles got a dose of the humiliation he so richly deserved.

"I don't care if Mr. Knowles is in conference," he told the startled receptionist. Raising his voice so anyone nearby would be sure to hear he said, "I'm investigating a homicide and I want Knowles now."

"Really," said Ed Knowles, ushering him hurriedly into an office so full of polished desks and tables it looked like a museum display. "I can't imagine what could be so important, Mr. Fields, that you'd call me out of a conference."

"Well, if you'd prefer it I could come to your apartment and talk in front of your wife," said Fields, grinning.

Knowles sighed. "Have a seat," he said. He sat behind his mammoth desk, in charge. "What have you come about?"

"Two things, Ed. Now, as you know I'm a Homicide cop. Normally I wouldn't bother with anything so mild as break and enter." A gratifying pallor crept over the culprit's face.

"I can't imagine what you're talking about," he said.

"Aw, Ed, you know, and I know, that you were behind the robbery at Mrs. Platt's."

"That's the silliest thing I've ever heard. Why on earth would I want to rob Monica?"

Fields let the question hover in the air. There was a large framed picture of Mrs. Knowles on the desk. She was a nice-looking woman, and one who would probably be horrified at her husband's actions.

"I repeat," said Knowles, trying for the upper hand, "why would I want to rob Monica? She has nothing I would want, and even if I did make a practice of stealing, it certainly wouldn't be from her."

"Well, that brings me to the second reason I'm paying this visit, Ed. I came to tell you that Terence Burgess isn't going ahead with that lawsuit, so you can breathe a little easier."

At last his composure was utterly broken. His mouth literally fell open and he slumped in his chair. "How did you? You *knew* him?"

"No, I didn't. Not until yesterday. Just chalk it up to good detective work, and your heavy-handed ways. By the way, I checked with the Twentieth, and they confirmed that the glass of the window was broken from the inside. I wouldn't want you to turn to a life of crime, because you're not very good at it."

"I didn't pick her lock or anything," Knowles said. "I just used the spare key that's kept by the chief of operations. I *am* the operations person on the Board."

He sounded like a normally obedient child trying to justify a spell of naughtiness. Another thought occurred to him, another gold star on his paper.

"We didn't know he was black," he said. "Honestly we didn't."

"He just wasn't rich enough, you thought. He didn't sound like the sort of go-getter you and 'Barn'—whose real name was Fred, by the way—wanted to see in the building."

"Give me a break," Ed Knowles muttered, but there was an honest plea in it. "I was going to think of a way to return Monica's stuff, and she didn't have to pay for the window's repair."

"What about the fear an old lady might feel? What about the way you bullied her to make her lie at the meeting in the lobby? What were you going to do about that?"

Knowles looked as if he might begin to whimper. "I'm not really such a bad guy," he said. "It would have been worse for Monica if she'd been successfully sued. She'd be bankrupt."

"Here's what you're going to do, Ed. I won't let it become

known that you're a dirtbag if you follow my instructions to the letter." Knowles sat up straighter. This was the kind of talk he liked. Every problem had a solution.

"You're going to return that stuff to Monica in person. You're going to apologize abjectly for the way you treated her, and you'd better make it sound real. Say you were so distraught you were temporarily insane, picturing that big lawsuit. Reassure her that the suit is dead, kaput, and there's nothing to fear."

A look of mutiny passed over Ed Knowles' boyish face, and then was replaced with one of resignation. He nodded. "Be sure you make her feel important," Fields said. "If you can do that, she'll never tell a soul."

Meekly Ed Knowles walked out with him to the elevator. The whole reception area was carpeted in priceless Persian, and the receptionist, dressed as expensively as any Park Avenue matron, reigned over her domain with absolute assurance. She pretended not to be listening or taking any note of Fields, which was why it gave him such a kick to clasp his companion's shoulder and say, in carrying tones: "So long, Ed. From now on keep your nose clean."

When she recounted her conversation with the street musician, Lucky, she felt webs closing around her with every word. She thought she might strangle by the time she got around to the stuff she now knew was damning. Damning to her and her nonexistent skills at eliciting information.

Her *mentor*, as she privately thought of Fields, in a not unironic light, was about to hit the ceiling when he realized she hadn't been able to get Lucky's real name, first and last. She had thought he'd be so pleased with the Tyrone Williams identification, but he seemed most interested in having her repeat, verbatim, Lucky's responses to her questions.

They were sitting in one of his cars, double-parked in front of the building. They had scoured Columbus for the musician, but he had no doubt gone back to his job in the mail room. The mail room where? Why hadn't she asked?

"I'm sorry I didn't find out where he worked," she said, "but I didn't want him to get suspicious." Out of the corner of her eye she saw Ernesto, who'd been taking the air near the little alcove where garbage was stacked on collection days, scurry to open the front door. Fay Spooner was approaching, loaded down with shopping bags.

"I wish Ernesto wouldn't do that," she said. "It only makes them think how nice a doorman would be."

"Let's not get sidetracked," reproved Fields. "What did he say next?"

She repeated Lucky's little earnest riff about how none of the rest of the Easter kids' pals had had a key, only Tyrone. She kept her eyes straight forward, observing the hordes who gamboled on the Avenue, blissful in the unnatural heat, fairly springing along in their name-brand sneakers. Where were they all going?

"What was his tone of voice when he said none of the others had a key?"

Sarah considered. "Fairly intense," she said, "but not overly so. I know it opens a whole new can of worms."

"Not necessarily," said Fields. "Go on, please."

When she told him about Lucky's urgency in wanting her to remember Tyrone's name for the police he used what Sarah had called the "f-word" until she'd been twenty-seven.

"Couldn't you use that SEARCH computer to find out his real name? You could run 'Lucky' through the street names and see who it matched up with."

"First of all," said Fields through clenched teeth, and then he halted abruptly and assumed an alert, pleasant expression. She followed his glance and saw Mrs. Strabinski leaning in at the window on her side, rather like a horse at a paddock.

"I've just now had a call from the Managing Agent," Ida said, smiling broadly. "Would February the nineteenth be convenient for you, Sarah?"

"For what?"

Ida clucked. "Shame, Sarah," she said. "Have you forgotten already? The *troika!* You and me and Monica! It's the next meeting of the new Board of Directors, if you agree."

Sarah said she was sure it would be all right, and her neighbor backed off, still smiling, and headed for Broadway. The sun, strong as only sun filtered through a thousand chemicals can be in a New York February, glinted from the police whistle Ida wore on a chain around her neck.

"You were saying?" Sarah asked.

"SEARCH isn't going to turn up any *Lucky* for a street name," he said furiously. "It's about a hundred years out of date. Probably Lucky Luciano was the last person to use it."

"Well, I'm really very sorry," said Sarah. "I admit I didn't handle it very well, but I don't have your *expertise*, and I can't see this creepy kid having any connection to Seawright at all."

"You didn't give him your name, did you?"

"No," said Sarah, "and he didn't remember me anymore than I remembered him." She thought it would be nice if Fields could imagine her in peril from the untalented street musician, but it didn't seem to be the case. Perhaps she was too honest, after all.

"And you didn't mention your apartment number, did you? That's very important, Sarah."

"Certainly not," she said in as distant and uninterested a voice as she could manage. "Lucky is not about to track me to the seventh floor and ring my bell and bash my brains in with his violin case." She drummed her nails against the dashboard, feeling sulky and perturbed. "If this weather holds, you should be able to pick him up tomorrow. It will be Valentine's Day, and I imagine he'll play some excruciating rendition of 'My Funny Valentine.'"

But Fields seemed determined not to be amused.

"Don't you try to run him down, Sarah," he said. "If you see him, don't speak to him or make any sign of recognition. Just walk on by. Will you do that for me?"

"I will," said Sarah, "but I don't see why. He's just an unappealing kid, don't you think?"

"I think he's a regular John the Baptist," said Fields. "He christened himself when he met you. You *were* his luck."

TWENTY

"Murderous Minstrel: *He Wanted To Have It All!*"

Maryanne snorted at the *Post*'s wrapup of the murder, and then slid it between two fragile dessert plates. Although she hadn't found a buyer yet, she was selling her apartment and moving back to New Jersey, where rents were more reasonable. She had begun her packing because she knew it would take weeks.

"He wasn't a minstrel," she said to Sarah Mason, who was helping her. "Don't minstrels have to sing?"

"I guess it sounded better than murderous mail room boy," said Sarah. "This has been a very downscale affair after all."

"But his motive was upscale, don't forget that."

The two women worked on, stripping Maryanne's apartment of all the things which had made it a home in the days of her marriage and which had lately been so wearisome to her.

It had all come round full circle of course, and just as Fields had said, everything was connected. The street musician had seen *his* opportunity back in January when the body appeared in the bookstore window. Leonard Muellen was his uncle, and Leonard Muellen had no one to leave his money to but the no-good son of his dead sister. The boy had once shown talent, but he had dropped out of Music and Art in the seventies and led the life of a parkie. He had always been a boy who was unwilling to look to the future, and the bookstore owner might have wished he had a more worthy heir, but in the end blood must have been stronger than good sense, and his will revealed that his entire estate was to go to Donald Muellen Frye.

Donnie had been found easily enough, though something in his encounter with Sarah had made him move his act to Amsterdam Avenue in the Eighties. He had not been playing "My Funny Valentine" but "Norwegian Wood," and when Fields had approached him he'd made the mistake of running. Even when caught, Donnie Frye swore ten ways from Sunday that he had had nothing to do with the death of Barnett Seawright. He tried to put Tyrone the Speechless forward as the killer, but it was he who was carrying a switchblade.

It was very easy to get him to talk, and the more silent the detective became the more voluble were Donnie Frye's explanations of why he was surely innocent. *He* had no key to the building, like freaked-out Tyrone; *he* had never needed to huddle in someone's fire stairs for warmth; *he* had never been homeless. If Fields thought he was some loser he was very much mistaken. Donnie didn't need latchkeys, because he had friends who would freely admit him to fancy apartments and penthouses. Well, maybe not penthouses exactly, but Fields was free to search the apartment he shared with his father in Brooklyn because he would never find any key to that building.

The silence with which he was greeted seemed to panic him, but it never occurred to him to be silent, as he'd been cautioned he had a right to be.

"I'll be coming into a lot of money soon," was something he repeated often. Fields didn't believe him until the computer check revealed his middle initial, "M," to stand for Muellen. Donnie could hardly deny his identity, and admitted that he was the nephew of the unfortunate bookstore owner. Uncle Lenny had left him all his money; he would be rich as soon as the will was probated. He would probably be moving into the neighborhood, buying his own co-op off Columbus Avenue when his money came through.

Fields finally allowed as how it *was* ridiculous to think that Donnie could have got into the building on the fatal day, because street musicians were never buzzed in, what with the security rules. "I didn't have to try to sneak into buildings, I keep *telling* you," he'd said in anguish. To prove his point, he admitted that he had been in the building last summer. Never on that day in January, but one summer night he had been *invited* in, to the penthouse no less, by Barnett Seawright himself. Seawright

had been coming out of that new Thai restaurant with two
women friends, and they had been laughing and laughing for
some reason, and the next thing he knew Seawright was offering
him twenty bucks to come up and serenade them on the penthouse roof.

"So you see," said Donnie virtuously, "I wouldn't have
wanted to kill a man like that. We were almost like *friends.*"

But something, perhaps the realization, long-buried until
now, that he had been invited up to the roof as a sort of after-
dinner joke, made Donnie begin to cry. Perhaps he believed that
forensic science was now so advanced that he had left fingerprints on the old fridge right through his gloves, or perhaps he
was tired of living with the memory. Whatever it was, Donnie
announced that it had been easy getting into that building. The
doors had been propped open to allow some delivery men in,
and he had just walked in as easy as anything. But he hadn't
gone to the laundry room. No. He had ridden up to the top floor
and then climbed the stairs he remembered to the penthouse. It
had been an impulse. Now that he knew he was going to be rich,
he had to think of the future, and the future would include
living in this neighborhood where everything was happening.
He thought Mr. Seawright, who had once invited him in, would
be able to let him know when anything came available in his
building.

But there'd been a small note taped to the door of the penthouse, advising that Mr. Seawright was in the storage room, so
Donnie had gone down to the basement. He'd found him not in
the storage room but in the laundry room, where he was examining the lock on an expensive racing bike. Seawright didn't
seem to recognize him, and when Donnie explained who he was
the man got angry and asked him what the hell he was doing in
the laundry room.

"I tried to explain, about my inheritance and everything, but
he just told me not to be a fool. He didn't actually curse me out
or call me names. It was more like I wasn't even *there.*"

Fields could see how it had been. Donnie had seen his dream,
the dream of a trivial mind, but a dream nonetheless, disinte-
grating. He would never get to live in an airy, gracious pent-

house with plants and trees and the lights of Manhattan wink-
ing and twinkling just for him. He would never get to live in a
building like this, because he wasn't important. Still, he wasn't
angry enough to lose control, not quite, until Seawright said
something so unforgivable Donnie had simply used the only
resource he had to punish him. Just before he turned his back,
dismissing Donnie forever, Barnett Seawright had looked him
in the eyes and said: "How many uncles do you have? Because
you'd need one to die every year for the rest of your life to
afford to live here."

And so the knife in the back, the frantic disposal in the old
fridge, and Donnie's numb exit from the building, passing unde-
tected among the deliverymen.

"I guess I was temporarily insane, huh?" he'd concluded, almost cheerfully. "One thing's for sure. This won't come to trial
for a long time, and by then I'll have my money. I'm going to
get the best lawyer that money can buy!"

On a bright Sunday morning in April, Columbus Avenue was
so packed with foot traffic it was hard to have an actual destina-
tion. Most of the strollers had none, and that was why they
inched along, looking in the windows of the shops, making sudden decisions to enter one and examine an amusing shirt or
desirable pair of boots.

The riot gates were permanently down at Food World, and
Maryanne's handiwork invisible to the gaping throngs. Raider's
had closed down and been replaced by yet another Chinese restaurant, A Wok on the Wild Side. O'Reilly's wore a "Lost Our
Lease" sign, and it was rumored that the new tenants were planning an imported soap and bath oil boutique.

None of these changes and portents mattered to the Sunday
crowds, who were, after all, simply killing time until brunch.

A young woman called Jill was trying to make good time,
battling against the crowds. She wanted to get to the flea market
on Seventy-seventh before all the good items were snapped up.
She had a passion for anything that was mysterious and exotic
and, above all, *authentic*. She had just moved into the parlor floor
of a brownstone between Central Park West and Columbus, and

she wanted to surround herself with evidence of a rich and well-traveled past. She'd nearly lost it when she saw her new neighbor's collection of rare and wonderful artifacts.

Her personal favorite was the intricately carved wooden sculpture Ben used as a door prop in his kitchen. It was painted in reds and blacks that hadn't come from any bucket of latex. Jill was sure they were dyes made from berries and roots, pure, natural sources, because Ben had assured her that the piece was very old. It had been, he said, the scepter of an African king.

Since he'd already told her of his travels and none of them had included Africa, Jill asked how he had acquired such a wondrous object.

She'd been afraid, to judge by the peculiar look he'd given her, that Ben was going to reveal an astonishing price paid to Sotheby's or some such place. He'd paused for a very long time before he revealed his source: the flea market. And at what a price—only fifteen dollars!

Jill could hardly believe his luck, and said so, but Ben had countered that the artifact was slightly scarred at one end and denuded of minute chips of color.

Jill saw that the only way she could possibly get to the flea market in time for the opening was to take a detour. She veered off Columbus and onto a side street, heading for Amsterdam. She would execute a perfect square and double back, avoiding the worst of the crowds. She would arrive at the flea market on time for the opening and—if fortune smiled on her—she would return to her new apartment bearing something of lasting value.

She imagined her treasure as an object she'd take with her, no matter how high she might soar. "Yes," she would say to her unborn grandchildren, "this has been with me since my earliest days in New York."

Manhattan was a glorious place, full of opportunity.

Mary Bringle is the author of eleven previous novels, and *Murder Most Gentrified* is her third for the Crime Club. She lives with her husband and son in a gentrified neighborhood in Manhattan, reluctantly.